PAYBACK JONNY'S REVENGE

BY

J. N. STEPHENSON

Copyright © J. N. Stephenson 2016
This book is sold subject to the condition that it shall not, by way of trade or otherwise, be lent, resold, hired out, or otherwise circulated without the publisher's prior consent in any form of binding or cover other than that in which it is published and without a similar condition including this condition being imposed on the subsequent publisher.
The moral right of J. N. Stephenson has been asserted.
ISBN-13: 978-1540339867
ISBN-10: 1540339866

DEDICATION

To my wife Karen who has supported me through the writing of this book and my four sons Dylan, Brad, Ky and Makenzie.

CONTENTS

CHAPTER 1 *Recovery* 1
CHAPTER 2 *Sam And His Crew* 6
CHAPTER 3 *Time To Plan* 11
CHAPTER 4 *The Shopping List* 15
CHAPTER 5 *My 1st Kill: Norman* 25
CHAPTER 6 *Detective Porter* 37
CHAPTER 7 *Hear No Evil* 48
CHAPTER 8 *Porter And The Deal* 59
CHAPTER 9 *50 Shades Of Black And Blue* 72
CHAPTER 10 *Bump And Run* 79
CHAPTER 11 *The Pickled Eggs* 90
CHAPTER 12 *The Red Lion And A Wee Dance* 104
CHAPTER 13 *24 Hours* 122
CHAPTER 14 *The Trip To Millisle* 128
CHAPTER 15 *The Strippers* 136
CHAPTER 16 *Charged* 144
CHAPTER 17 *Sam's Money* 159
CHAPTER 18 *Eye To Eye* 172
CHAPTER 19 *It Could Have Been Me* 182
CHAPTER 20 *On The Run* 190
CHAPTER 21 *Closer* 201
CHAPTER 22 *The Warm Sun* 214

This is a work of fiction. Names, characters, businesses, organizations, places, events and incidents either are the product of the author's imagination or are used fictitiously. Any resemblance to actual persons, living or dead, events, or locales is entirely coincidental.

CHAPTER 1

Recovery

The blue lights got brighter, the sirens got louder and then all went quiet. I must have passed out. When I came round, I was lying in the back of an ambulance hooked up to a drip with wires attached to my chest.

"Back with us son."

I heard a man say, I turned my head to see a paramedic sitting beside me. As the speeding ambulance rushed to get me to hospital, I floated in and out of consciousness and when I came round I saw the bright lights of the hospital corridor. As I was rushed to surgery I heard a voice say, "He's lost a lot of blood, his right leg is a clean puncture but his left leg has a severe laceration and possible ricochet into the lower abdomen."

I passed out again and the next thing I knew, I was lying in a ward and my mum was holding my hand.

"Jonny son, you're back, can you hear me son?"

I couldn't speak; I had a tube down my throat which I tried to remove. My mum held my hand to stop me and said,

"Leave it son it's to help you breathe, I will get a doctor."

I nodded my head and laid there, as I watched my mum go and get a nurse a tear travelled down my cheek at the realization of what had happened. The image of Gerrard's face was etched in my mind forever.

My mum came back with a nurse who came over and sat beside me.

"Jonny, I am Paula, I am here to look after you, you have come through quite a lot and are very lucky to be alive son. We will get the tube removed shortly but just relax and just remember your safe here, nobody can hurt you anymore, I will be back soon."

I nodded my head and just laid holding my mum's hand.

After a while a doctor came with two other young doctors and they pulled the curtain round. The doctor introduced himself, "Hi Jonny, I am Doctor Beck, I took care of you when you came in. These are junior doctors, is it ok if they stay while I remove your tube?"

I nodded my head.

The doctor held my chest and slowly pulled the tube out, I gagged and coughed as it was pulled out of my throat, tears travelled down my cheeks but for the first time I was able to breathe on my own.

Dr Beck then said, "Well Jonny, how are you feeling?"

"I am very sore, my legs, my belly and my throat all hurt."

As I coughed, I winced in pain and held my stomach.

"We will get you something for the pain but to be honest son, you are a very lucky boy. By the time we got you on the surgery table, you had lost a lot of blood one, of the bullets that you were shot with travelled up into your lower abdomen and it was a very long procedure to get it removed and repair the damage. You have been in intensive care now for 5 days and to be honest, I only gave you 50/50% chance of surviving so to get to this stage is superb but it's not going to be easy. You're going to have to learn to walk again and maybe have another operation as we might need to go in again to do a clean-up, but we won't know until we scan you then we will decide what's needed."

I lay there not knowing what to think, I looked at my mum and she was crying.

"Mum it will be ok, I don't give up easy so stop crying."

I held her hand really tightly and just smiled at her.

"So Jonny, first thing is first, let's get you some pain relief and I will be back later to check on you."

"Thanks doctor, thanks for everything you have done."

"No problem Jonny, just promise me one thing, keep that fighting spirit up and we will get you back fighting fit."

At that the doctors left and they pulled the curtains back, to my amazement, Karen was standing there.

She had the biggest smile I had ever seen, she walked over and threw her arms round me. It was the best feeling in the world, when she hugged me the pain was horrific but I didn't care, I held her so tight, I was so glad just to see her again as I thought I never would.

"Jonny, how are you?" she asked.

"All the better for seeing you," I replied.

"I see you haven't lost your wit, so you must be ok."

"Aye I'm ok just a bit sore."

"Karen, love, don't listen to him, he isn't out of the woods yet, they might need to do another operation and he is to go through a lot of physio to get him walking again so he is going to be in for a few weeks yet."

"Seriously Mrs Andrews? Oh my God, that's terrible," Karen replied.

Just at that, a nurse came in with tablets for me to take.

"I'm really sorry ladies but you are going to have to leave, Jonny needs to rest."

"Can they not stay a little bit longer?" I asked.

"No Jonny, I am really sorry but we have to get you comfortable and these tablets are quite strong so they will probably make you sleep."

"Jonny it's ok, I will be back tomorrow to see you," Karen replied.

"I know son, you need to rest, I will see you tomorrow night," my mum said.

And at that, Karen kissed me and they left.

I took the tablets and the nurse was right, within 30 minutes I was out like a light.

As I dreamed all I could see was the bastard's faces that tortured Gerrard and killed him and put me here in hospital. I went through so many scenarios in my head about killing them and a flash and loud bang and I woke with a jerk, it was dark and I lay there in bed thinking of Sam and his crew and it was that moment I knew I wanted revenge.

The days past so slowly, I didn't need another operation and physio was hard but my determination kept me going. I was able to walk a few steps unaided after about 10 days and I grew stronger and stronger. Eventually after 3 weeks, I got home and made plans to meet Billy and see how the land laid with Sam, and maybe get back to work.

CHAPTER 2

Sam And His Crew

It was a few days later, I went to see Billy, it was a Monday night which I knew would be a good time to speak with him because it was darts night. It didn't start until 8pm so at 6.30 I sat in my car waiting for Billy to turn up and when he did it was like old times, we just fell into the same routine.

"Alright Jonny lad, are you here to give me a hand?"

"I need to speak with you Billy, can we go inside?"

"Yes Jonny, come on and we will get a wee pint to celebrate you coming back to work."

We walked into the bar and it was the same old smell, same old chairs and tables but one thing had changed, the two holes in the middle of the floor were still there and it sickened me as I knew why they were there. It made me more determined to get back and gain the confidence of Sam and his Hench men so I could be trusted again and become invisible.

Billy poured two pints and set them over on one of the tables.

"Grab a seat Jonny, it's been a while since I have seen you, how's the legs son?"

"Getting there Billy, still sore in the mornings but when I take my tablets it's fine."

"That's good son, so what can I help you with?"

"Billy it's Sam and the rest of them Bastards, what am I going to do?"

"Nothing son, there is absolutely nothing you can do, I hope when the peelers interviewed you that you took my advice and said nothing."

"Aye I did Billy but there was this one detective, he was really pushy, he was called detective Porter and to be honest he wouldn't take no for an answer. He came back to the hospital about four times but I kept telling him what you told me to say, that I didn't recognise any of them as they were wearing masks and that they said they were from the I.R.A. He seemed to buy that but he kept asking and wondering why they didn't shoot me in the head and why they killed a Catholic."

"That's good son, that goes in your favour with Sam but we will need to set up a meeting with him to know for sure."

Just at that the door swung open, as I had my back to the door I didn't know who had walked in but the look on Billy's face said it all, I knew it was Sam.

"Just the man I have been looking for."

I turned round and there standing in the middle of the floor was Sam and Jonty, my heart stopped, I had a big lump in my throat and I turned a few shades of white. I was scared, really scared, I didn't know what to say. I stood up and just stared at them, I knew in that split moment this was it, if they were going to finish the job this was their chance.

"Sit down Jonny we are only here to talk," Sam said.

I walked round to the other side of the table and sat down with my back to the wall, Sam and Jonty sat down opposite Billy and me, Billy spoke up,

"Sam, you know and I know what happened to Jonny was bang out of order."

"I will stop you there Billy, it should never have happened but you got to understand we are living in dangerous times and to be honest I didn't know who I could trust but I need to know Jonny, what did you tell the peelers?"

"Nothing Sam, I am not that stupid, I would never tout on any one."

At that Jonty laughed.

"You're a fucking ball bag, you were talking with that *taig* and feeding him our information."

"You're wrong Jonty, I only knew him through football, we played at the milk cup and that's the only reason I knew him."

"Enough Jonty, we can only take Jonny at his word and what I say is final. I believe Jonny and you Jonty, you're a lucky boy I didn't nut you for what you done on him so it's time to call an end to the internal bickering, we have bigger things that need taking care of."

And at that Sam reached into his inside pocket of his coat, it was like something out of the movies. It was like time stood still as he pulled out an envelope, I was holding my breath and then gave a sigh of relief when it wasn't a gun.

"Here Jonny, this is for you, it is a good will payment to make things easier for you and in the way of an apology for what happened."

I took the envelope off Sam, it was like blood money but I knew if I refused it that he would take offence and I would probably end up in one of Bates' skips.

We all stood up and Sam said, "Right that's that sorted, now Jonty you bury the hatchet and forget about this whole thing."

Jonty stood there with his hand out but I knew rightly that he would rather bury the hatchet in my head, and to be honest as I stood there staring at him I could see in my mind the blood running out of his eyes and visualising him taking his last breath. It was only for a few seconds but it was so clear in my mind that when I blinked the vision was gone, I shook his hand as I also grinded my teeth and squeezed his hand tightly as he squeezed mine, in that moment I think we both knew we had unfinished business.

Sam and Jonty left and Billy said to me, "Well that's it settled then, you're back to work."

He didn't even mention the envelope, he just got on with getting the bar set up for the darts team. I went about my usual work as well but it was when I was lighting the fire I got flash backs of Gerrard and his face, it made me angry and under my breath I told myself, "I will get them, I will get every last fucking one of them."

The dart team started arriving and it was a cup game so there was a half decent crowd in so the night went by quickly. I was glad to be back to work and back to my old routine, a few of the regulars were in as well so there was a bit of crack and a few drinks as well, it was what I needed. I had to try and get on with my life but most important was that I was now getting close to Sam again and that I had to start making plans to execute them all.

.

CHAPTER 3

Time To Plan

After work when I got home I went straight to bed. I lay awake all night planning on how I would execute Sam and his whole crew, I knew it would be difficult but I had the upper hand now with Sam taking me back under the wing of the U.F.F so I could use that to get close to them and find out their movements. But it was how I was going to get to each and every one of them that was the hard bit, but in my mind I planned that each one of them had to suffer like Gerrard did and that's where my plan started.

After my mum left the house to go to her wee cleaning job, I counted the money Sam had gave me, 3 grand was in it and I thought it was a cheap price to pay for Gerrard's life but each one of those pounds I would use to get my revenge. My first part of my plan was to get a lock up somewhere quiet and a van as well so off I went to get the Telegraph to see if there was anywhere suitable, I sat in my car going through the ads and bingo, a farmer had an outbuilding for rent up Blackmountain, I drove straight to it.

When I arrived it was exactly what I needed, a secluded lane, only one way in and out and no one near me for a mile or so. I rang the number straight away and the guy said he would come and meet me.

About 30 minutes passed and a car pulled up, a big lump of a man got out of an awl rust bucket of a car and walked over, I got out of the car and shook his hand.

"I take it you're Brian?" the man said.

"Yes I am," as I shook his hand, "I never caught your name?"

"It's Paddy and could you tell me what you want the building for?"

"I am a furniture collector, I buy the odd bit at the auction and restore it and knock it on for a few quid but I need a place to work as the place I have now isn't big enough. Your building is just what I am looking for, how much is the rent for 6 months?"

"I love to hear a young man making a go at something, it's not every day I meet a young business man, would £100 a month do you?"

"Yes that would be perfect."

I reached into my pocket and lifted out £200 that I had brought and handed it to Paddy, we shook hands and that was it sorted. As I stood there watching paddy drive back down the lane, I was really pleased with myself and took a walk round the building to get a feel for it and what I needed to change.

As I went into the main room of the building, it had a few electric points, and one single bulb hung from the centre of the room. I found the light switch and turned it on, as I stood there in the middle of the room I got a real feel for it, it was perfect, no windows, a low ceiling and great big thick walls so really quiet. It had an awl fireplace at one end of the room and a table and two chairs that had seen better days, but the main thing for me was that it had only one door in and out with a great big bolt and padlock which Paddy had gave me the key for so it was exactly what I needed to carry out my plan.

I locked up and got back into my car, I sat there looking at the ads in the Telegraph and one jumped out at me, a 10 year old *Ford* transit with low miles and a full service history, but then I read on, it had 6 months tax and M.O.T and for the measly price of £650 I thought, that's the van for me. I got on the phone and spoke to the guy about it, he still had it and it was only over on the falls road so I drove to meet him.

When I arrived my first impressions was that it was a rust bucket but he assured me that it was a great wee driving van so I gave it a test drive and he was right, the awl thing drove well. I remembered the checks Billy had shown me with my car so when I had a good hoke round the engine, I was happy enough. I said to the man,

"What's the least you will take for it mate?"

"I couldn't take any less than £600, so if you want it that's what you will buy it for."

I put my hand out and said, "Your word is good

enough mate."

As we shook hands I gave him 50 quid and told him I would call the next day with the rest.

The next morning, I got a taxi over to pick the van up and as the man gave me the keys he said,

"I need your details to send the registration book away, can you write them down for me?"

He handed me the registration book and pointed to where I had to fill in, I wrote my name as Andrew Wright, I lived in 14 Dover Street and signed the bottom of the section. He was happy enough and even gave me a tenner back for a lucky penny and off I went to hide the van up at the building.

It took me about 40 minutes to walk back down home but it gave me time to think about equipment and who my first target was going to be.

CHAPTER 4

The Shopping List

Over the next few days I got together all the items I needed for the job I had in front of me, a hammer, cable ties, nails, a saw, 2 heavy duty car batteries with jump cables, needle and thread, a set of butcher knives, a steel chair, garden secateurs and a blow torch. The last thing was quite hard to find but it was when I went to an auction house to get the chair, I saw it, an engraving machine that was used to engrave trophies, it reminded me of the time I won the school's cup and held the trophy above my head when we celebrated so I was really pleased to have found it. I got all the gear set up in the room and made sure the chair was firmly bolted to the floor with 4 big brackets.

I got to work on my first part of the plan to engrave the names of Sam and his crew onto a bullet for each one of them bastards and it was a bit nerve wrecking but I took my time. After about 2 hours' work, I had it done, as I lay each of the five bullets on the table they reflected the light and they shone like stars in the sky. I looked at my watch and knew I had to be home for my tea, as I drove down the road the rain came on and it was pelting down. I had to slow down and turn my window wipers on full just to try and see the road, it took me ages to get home, the rain just didn't let up. The roads turned into rivers and within those 20 minutes or so, the Shankill road had turned into a river, I swear if you had a canoe you could have paddled into town but I pulled up outside my house and bolted in through the front door.

As I got in my nanny was sitting on the sofa with her head in her hands.

"What's wrong nanny?" I said.

She stood up and threw her arms around me.

"Oh Jonny, it's your mum, she's gone."

"What do you mean nanny, gone where?"

"Jonny she was knocked down going to the shop at the Woodvale."

My heart sunk.

"Nanny where is she, is she ok?"

"No son she isn't, she died lying on the road, she didn't stand a chance."

I stood there hugging my nanny crying like a wee child, I couldn't control myself, I fell to the floor. My mum had been going to the shops to get something in for our tea, when she went to cross the road, and with the heavy rain, a black taxi didn't see her and hit her straight on. She died instantly, my mum was taken away from me and my heart was so sore, my tears I couldn't stop. As my nanny sat beside me in our wee house, the two of us just hugged and cried.

In-between sobbing, I said to my nanny, "Nanny what are we going to do? Mum's gone, what are we to do?"

She looked up at me, "Jonny son, there is nothing we can do. My Annie and you is all I had left, you both were my life, I don't know what to say son."

My nanny was in her 80s, she was a wee frail women and I was scared this could be the death of her so I put my both arms round her and said, "Nanny we still have each other, I will look after you, where is my ma now?"

She again wiped the tears from her eyes, "She is down in the Mater son, we have to go down to identify her body."

"When nanny, when do we have to go down?" I said as I wiped my tears away.

"We can go down later son but I don't know if I can."

"Nanny we have to, we have to do this together, I couldn't go on my own."

"Ok son, we will go down now."

Just at that a knock came to the door, I opened it up and Billy was standing there. I stood just looking at him with tears in my eyes.

"Jonny son, I just heard about your mum, I am so sorry son, is there anything I can do?"

"Yes Billy could you take my nanny and me down to the Mater hospital? We have to identify my mum's body."

"Of course son, anything you need, I'm here for you."

And at that my nanny lifted her coat and we got into Billy's car and made the short journey down the Crumlin Road to go to the Mater.

I sat in the front alongside Billy and out of the corner of my eye I could see my wee nanny sitting in the back crying into her hanky. I turned to face her, "Nanny are you ok?"

"Yes son, just can't believe my Annie is gone."

I couldn't say anything, I just sat there looking out the side window of Billy's car and at the faces of people that we passed, on the now what seemed to be an eternity, of a drive to the hospital. When we arrived we parked on the Crumlin Road and walked in. Billy did all the talking, I heard him say that we were here to identify Mrs Andrews' body that had been knocked down and killed on the Shankill road. I just stood there with my arm round my nanny trying to comfort her.

The girl behind the desk pointed towards a corridor that we had to go through and we started the long walk down. As I looked up at one of the signs, it read mortuary so I knew it was real. My nanny couldn't walk that well so it took a while to reach the door that we had to go through. A man stood at a desk just opposite and I heard Billy repeat what he said about identifying my mum's body, the man introduced himself as Jonathan and gave his condolences, he opened the door and ushered us in. I kept a good hold on my nanny as she was now really sobbing and as we walked into the room there was a single trolley with a white sheet on it covering my mum's body. We walked over and Jonathan pulled the sheet back, I just stood there, my mum was dead, she looked like she was just sleeping not a mark on her face. I leant over her and put my arms round her kissing her on the cheek, I cried as I said to her, "Mum I love you, it's not fair that you're gone, it's not fair." When I kissed her, she was so cold but just looked like she was sleeping. At that I heard a thump and it was like slow motion, I turned to see my nanny on the floor, Billy and Jonathan both went to her aid.

I couldn't move I was frozen to the spot, then I heard Billy shout at me, "Jonny get help," at that it was like a wakeup call, all of a sudden everything was so clear. I ran out the door screaming for help and at that two doctors came running down the hall, they pushed past me and went straight to my nanny.

Jonathan took Billy by the arm and brought him over to me he said, "Stay here, let the doctors do their work." He then ran up the corridor to get more help as Billy and me stood there looking in at the two doctors trying to revive my nanny. We were numb we didn't speak a word, we just looked on in vain as the doctors were pumping my nanny's chest and breathing into her mouth.

I could just hear one of them counting, "One, two, three, four, five, breathe" and again and again until I saw another nurse come running down with a trolley and a machine on it.

The doctor lifted two pads with wires attached to them and placed them on my nanny's chest, he turned the machine on and said, "Set, clear," and he pressed a button. As my nanny's body lifted off the ground, he leant over her again and checked her heart beat, he said, "No response, set again," and again he said, "Clear," and my nanny's body lifted off that cold tiled floor. He leant down and checked and looked round at me, he shook his head and Jonathan closed the door.

I fell to the floor just holding my head, I didn't cry, I just was in shock as Billy put his arm round me I could just hear him say, "Jonny, Jonny, Jonny." I looked up but it was just ringing in my ears, the same ringing as when I got blew across the street in the Shankill bomb. I just looked at Billy, I could see his lips move but couldn't hear a word, he helped me to my feet and ushered me over to a seat where we sat down.

After a while, the doctors and nurse came out of the room, one of them came over, I looked at him as he started talking, I couldn't hear anything but ringing but knew by looking at him that he was telling me my nanny had died.

When the doctor left, Billy put his arm round me and helped me up and we walked to his car. I couldn't breathe, I thought to myself, this couldn't be real, I was telling myself to wake up it had to be a dream but real it was. I sat in Billy's car, I was numb, in one awful day I had lost my mum and nanny and felt I couldn't continue, life was killing me, I was left on my own.

Billy drove me up home and stayed a while, we talked about the funeral arrangements and he said he would arrange it all. I swear if it wasn't for Billy in my life, I wouldn't be here.

Both funerals were on the same day, my mum and nanny were carried down the Shankill road side by side and again the turnout of people was huge. I was absolutely useless, I was in bits and it was only for Karen and her family helping that I got through that day.

When we got back after the crematorium where both my nanny and mum got cremated, Billy had laid on sandwiches and tea for everyone. The amount of people that came over to give me their condolences was unbelievable but it was when Sam and his crew stood in front of me and said sorry to hear about my mum and nanny that I stood up. Sam shook my hand and said, "If there is anything you need Jonny, just ask."

In my head I thought, yes there is, the five of you bastards tied up in the back of my van and me driving you to my kill room, but in reality I said, "It's ok, Billy has everything sorted." As I looked over to Jonty he stood there with that same smirk on his face as if to say he liked to see me suffer and in constant pain. I just looked back at him and again the vision was as clear as day, the blood running from his eyes and him gasping for breath, for a brief moment it was so real and then blink it was gone.

I sat back down again as another man came walking over and set a pint in front of me, "Here son get that down you." As he set the pint in front of me he said, "I'm sorry to hear about your mum and nanny, I am sure this is a hard day for you but if you need anything don't hesitate to ask."

"Thanks, that means a lot."

In fact, I got quite a few pints set in front of me and by the end of the night I was blind drunk and could hardly walk. Karen and her family went home early so I was sort of glad as I didn't want Karen to see the state I was in. Billy made sure I got home and stayed overnight to make sure I was ok and didn't do anything stupid.

The next morning, I woke with a banging headache, I swear every noise was deafening and I couldn't stop being sick. Even when Billy gave me two tablets and a glass of water, as soon as they hit my stomach, a quick dash to the toilet and up they came again. In fact, even after I puked up the awl yellow bile, when I was sick it just hurt as nothing was left in my stomach to bring up. I just spent the day on the settee absolutely ill and with memories of the previous day, I cried a few times and felt scared about how I was to deal with being on my own. Billy left about lunch time and the house was so quiet, I fell asleep and didn't wake until the early hours of the next morning.

I made myself a cup of tea and some toast but after a few mouthfuls, I couldn't eat anymore as I still felt sick. I sat on the settee thinking about how to get on with life and it was a hard choice to make, do I try and forget about Sam and his crew and try and build a life with Karen? But it still haunted me about what they had done and I still felt that we had un-finished business, or do I finish the plan I had in place? But what about Karen? I couldn't have her involved, she didn't deserve to be dragged into my fight and to be honest, if Sam got to her, it would devastate me, so I had to make a big choice.

After a couple of hours going back and forth about what to do, walking the floors, I had made my mind up and it was to finish the job off and execute them bastards, so I had to break up with Karen and not get her caught up in my plan.

The next couple of days I spent getting my nanny's house cleared out and it was handy that I had my van and somewhere to store her furniture. It was a good cover to have her furniture up at my rented farm buildings, but it was when I was clearing her bedroom out that I found in the bottom of her wardrobe a shoe box. As I sat on the edge of her bed, I slowly opened it up, at first there was some old photos but at the bottom of the box there was four bundles of money. My eyes lit up, I sat and counted it and it came to six thousand pounds, it must have been my nanny's life savings so I quickly put it back in the box and walked out and hid it behind my seat in the van.

After a few hours I had the house cleared, Billy turned up in the afternoon to give me a hand with the furniture and cooker to take to the charity shop and it was on our way down the Shankill. He said to me, "Well Jonny, are you wanting to come back to work yet or do you need more time off?"

"I need to get back to work Billy, I can't stand being in the house anymore so if you don't mind I will be back tonight."

"Aye that's great Jonny, I have missed you in work, it's not the same without you."

When we got back after leaving the furniture at the charity shop, Billy said he would see me later on about 6.30. I waved him off and locked my nanny's house for the last time then posted the keys through the letter box as the council were to get the house back the following day. I sat in my van for a minute and said goodbye to her wee house, noticing the chunk still missing from the door frame and I gave a wee smile to myself on the memories it had left me as a young boy growing up and visiting her on a Sunday.

On the drive back up Blackmountain, I began to plan my first hit, who it should be and, more importantly, when.

CHAPTER 5

My 1st Kill: Norman

It was 6.20pm, I drove down to work to open up with Billy but I knew tonight there would be a committee meeting so I wanted to be the one to stay behind and pour the drinks, and more importantly be able to lock up and start to put together my plan to get Norman. I needed to know his movements and the best place to grab him and put him in the back of my van.

The usual set up with the darts was due to finish around 10, the usual men came in and sat in the same seats in the same order and at 10.30, Jonty told everyone to leave. That was my cue, I turned to Billy. "Billy if you want to head on, I will lock up tonight, you haven't had an early night in ages so I don't mind staying back."

"Brilliant Jonny, I am cream crackered, it's great to have you back, I could do with an early one. Could you come in tomorrow for 4? We have a delivery."

"Yeah, no worries, see you then." I couldn't get Billy out quick enough as I needed to watch and listen to everything Norman was saying and more importantly, anywhere he was due to go.

I kept myself quite close to where Norman was sitting trying to listen to what he was saying, but there was nothing of real interest. Sam was doing all the talking about money and who was short on their pickups but it was when he said to Norman, "Norman, I need you to send a message to Roy from Wilton Street, he hasn't paid in 4 weeks now so you need to deal with this directly. Do it late on, he is usually back in from work around 1am so it will be quiet and nobody should be about. I want you to go solo on this one as you haven't to mess about," at that my ears pricked up.

"No worries Sam, I will call tomorrow night."

Just at that Jonty looked up at me, "Pour some drinks ballbag, my mouth is as dry as a Fenians face cloth." That got a laugh from the rest of the men sitting there, me, I just glared at him. In my head I was saying, "Your time will come," and I gave a wee smile and turned and walked to the bar to pour the drinks. As I stood behind the bar, my mind was racing, I was to start this tomorrow night.

The rest of the night I stood behind the bar, I wasn't even interested in what they were talking about, just couldn't wait to get the night over. It was bloody 1.30am before they decided to leave and as I pulled the shutter down and locked it and walked to my car, Jonty was standing at it. I stopped in my tracks and just stood there looking at him.

"What's wrong, cat got your tongue?" he said, I just glared at him, he was an evil bastard, I knew what he meant when he mentioned tongue and he knew what buttons to press with me.

"Fuck off Jonty, I don't want any trouble just leave me alone," I said.

"Oh, I won't leave you alone until you're in the ground beside that I.R.A bastard so believe me when I tell you this, when Sam is gone and I run things, your 1st on my list and there will be nobody to stop me." I don't know what came over me, I just lunged at him, I grabbed him two handed by the throat as I walked forward with him in my grasp until he hit the railings outside the club I said to him, "You listen to me you fucking cunt, see when you come for me have the balls to come alone and make sure you finish me off cause if you don't I will definitely come back for you, and trust me when I tell you this, I will slice your throat from ear to ear and watch you take your last breath." He struggled to try and break free, he was turning purple and to be honest I could of just strangled him to death there and then but I had other plans for him and this would be too nice of a death, so I loosened my grip. As he gagged for breath, I punched him square in the face and he fell to the ground, as he lay there gasping for breath I leant down low and spoke really softly, "Remember when you come for me, I will be waiting."

I left him lying in the street and got into my car, as I drove up home my adrenaline was amazing, I was buzzing. The power I had, the feeling, was like no other, I loved it and wanted more. When I got home, I went straight to bed but I couldn't sleep, I tossed and turned all night and couldn't wait for morning to come.

When I got up there were many things going round my head but the most important thing was Karen and how I was going to break up with her. It was about 10.30am and I rang her, the very sound of her voice made everything ok but I knew I couldn't drag her into my now world of revenge and as I knew it was her day off, I arranged to pick her up and go for lunch.

As I drove over to her house in East Belfast, it was the longest drive ever, what was I going to say to her? How was I going to tell her that we were over? But as I pulled up outside her house, my heart was so heavy, I sounded the horn and she came out through her front door. She smiled at me and for a brief moment, all my troubles were forgotten about, I could just see how beautiful she was and how much I was in love with her but I had to bottle all that up. I just smiled back as she walked down her pathway and got into the car. "Hi Jonny, you look worried, what's up?"

Karen could read me like a book, I couldn't hide anything from her and that convinced me that I had to end it as she would know I was up to something and I couldn't take the chance on Sam getting to her. "Nothing Karen, just had a late night in work, where would you like to go for lunch?"

"Jonny there is something wrong and I am not going anywhere until you tell me."

"Karen this is the hardest thing I have had to do in my life and I hope you understand."

"What Jonny, what is it?" she said, very worried.

"Karen I am in a really bad place at the minute and need to sort some things out, I need to get my head clear and I need a few weeks to do it."

"What do you mean Jonny, are you in any trouble?"

"No Karen, I need some time to think, just to get my head straight."

"So what are you saying, you want a break from us?" I could see in her eyes she was really concerned and her eyes filled up with tears.

"Yes Karen, just for a few weeks." I held my breath and fought back the tears, this felt worse than losing both my mum and dad and even my nanny but I knew I had to do it.

"Jonny I am here for you if you need time, take all the time you need, I love you and I understand you need to be alone for a while so just pick up the phone anytime you want to talk." The tears were now flowing down Karen's cheeks and she leant over and kissed me on the cheek. She got out of the car and walked back in through her front door, I drove off, now with tears running down my cheeks. I was in bits and could hardly see the road on the drive home.

By the time I got home I had stopped crying and could now concentrate on getting my plan together.

I was now so focused on what needed to be done, so about 3.30 I drove up to my lock up and picked up the van. All what I needed, I had already put in the back so it was about 4 o'clock when I got back down the Shankill and parked the van in Wilton Street. It was a dead end street so I faced the van back up the way so it would be a quick getaway. I didn't know what house Norman was to call at so I parked about 5 houses down. I got out and locked up and started walking to work as I had to meet Billy for the delivery.

When I arrived up at Heather Street, the delivery truck was already there and Billy had started hand balling the crates in. "Oh, here's your man now, just in time too," Billy said as he looked over at me.

"Sorry Billy I had some stuff to do," I replied.

"It's ok Jonny, you're here now."

I got stuck into carrying the rest of the delivery in, it took about 45 minutes but we got it all in and into the store room. We sat down in the bar, Billy said to me, "Have you had any tea yet Jonny?"

"No mate, I didn't get a chance, what would you like, my shout?"

"Jesus Jonny are you not feeling well? You're buying dinner? Well if that's the case I will take a fish super and since you're paying, get me a portion of mushy peas and put extra vinegar on them."

"Spot on Billy, I will be back in a tick," and at that I went down to the chippy to get our tea.

It didn't take long and when I returned, Billy had a couple of pints pulled and he said to me, "We got this new beer in to try, it's called Kilkenny, see what you think."

I looked at it, it was a dark brown colour just a bit lighter than Guinness but I gave it a go, I took a big drink of it, I didn't know what to think, Billy looked at me and said, "Well what do you think?"

"Stinking Billy, how could anyone drink that? It tastes like crap."

Billy just laughed, "I thought the same Jonny but the rep tells me it's a winner all over town so we will test it out tonight on the punters."

I walked to the bar and lifted two tins of *Coke* and brought them over. "Here Billy, nothing as nice as fish and chips and a tin of *Coke*."

Billy laughed, "You're right there Jonny,' as he shovelled in a spoon full of mushy peas. "And these peas are great, I'd hate to smell me later," he laughed again.

The times I spent with Billy were really good, he treated me like his son rather than just someone who worked for him. I just wished I could have told him what I was going to do, but I knew he would have freaked and talked me out of it, so the less he knew, the better.

We finished our tea and got ready to open up, it was a really quiet night, just a few punters in and it dragged by. I swear every time I looked at the clock it had stopped and at 11pm, Billy called last orders and we had them all out for 11.30. As Billy locked up, he asked if I wanted a lift home but I refused and told him I was going to get something to eat out of the kebab shop so I waved him off and started the walk home. My heart was thumping and my mind racing, I was so excited at the thought of getting Norman. I got in through the front door of my wee house and couldn't put the time in quick enough, when the clock read 12.30 I began the walk down to Wilton Street. It took me about 30 minutes and when I got to my van, I noticed a man walk into his house just opposite to where I had parked. I put 2 and 2 together and that must have been Roy that Norman was to pay a visit to.

So I opened up the side door and got inside, as I crouched down just able to see up the street I sat and watched and waited for Norman. My heart was thumping, the hammer I had in my hand felt like a ton weight, I was shaking a bit I don't know if it was out of fear or excitement, I just couldn't wait for Norman to turn up. Just at that moment, I saw a figure turn into the street, I couldn't make him out as the street lights where really dim but as he got closer, I saw that it was Norman. He now was about 20 feet away, then 10 feet away, I had seconds to react, I coughed to get his attention and said softly, "Help, someone help me." At that, Norman poked his head into the side of the van and *smack,* I hit him across the head with the hammer, he fell into the van and *smack,* I hit him again. He was knocked out and I grabbed him by his jacket and pulled him into the van. I instantly cable tied his hands together and his feet, I turned him onto his back and shoved a rag into his mouth and put tape round his now bleeding head to keep him quiet. I poked my head out of the van to see if anyone had heard me but result, the street was empty and so quiet. I got out and got into the driver's side and started the drive up to my lock up, on the way up I could hear Norman moaning in the back, he was kicking the side of the van but at this time of the morning the roads where empty and I knew nobody but me could hear him.

The closer I got to my lockup, the more excited I got, I loved this feeling, my adrenaline was buzzing, I felt untouchable. I could hear Norman's moans get softer, he must have passed out, so the next 5 minutes was just me and my thoughts. When I arrived up at the lockup, I turned the van so that the side door was close to the front door of my kill room. I turned the engine off and got out, I didn't know what to expect when I opened the side door, when I did Norman was just lying in a heap, not moving so I grabbed him by the feet and pulled him forward he was heavy. Norman must have been 6ft tall of a slim build but trying to move him, I hadn't thought about, there was no way I could have carried him in so I left him there and walked round the other derelict farm building to see if there was anything I could use and bingo, an aul wheel barrow with the tyre still pumped up. When I returned to the van, Norman hadn't moved so I positioned the wheel barrow against the side of the van and pulled Norman into it. He didn't even flinch, he must have still been unconscious. I wheeled him into my room and struggled but eventually after about three goes, I got him into the seat which was in the middle of the room just under the single light that barley lit it. As I stood back and admired my handy work, I was really proud of what I had done but this was only the beginning, I cut the cable ties from Norman's hands and feet and strapped him to the chair.

He still didn't move, I gave him a couple of slaps to the face to try and wake him up but I got no reaction, I started taking the tape off from around his head and it was when the last bit came of the rag in his mouth came with it, I saw that it was soaking, I looked closer at it, it was soaked with blood. I instantly looked at Norman and blood was coming from his mouth, I shook him. "Wake up you Bastard, wake up." I shook him and shook him but his head just fell forward, I stood back and was furious he was dead, he had choked to death on his own blood.

"Bastard," I shouted, "you're fucking dead, you're fucking dead." I just stood there in disgust, I couldn't finish what I had planned and it angered me but I still had a job to do, I walked to the bench I had set up and lifted the bullet with Norman's name on it and then went over to Norman. I placed the bullet in his left nostril, I pushed it up but no matter how hard I pushed, the bullet was still only half way in and I wanted it all the way. Just the base of it was showing, so to my wisdom I decided to hit it with a hammer to send it home but the outcome was not what I expected. As I took a couple of practice swings, I honestly didn't see the outcome, on the 3rd swing I struck the bullet and BANG the fucking thing went off and took half of Norman's head with it. It scared the crap out of me, I jumped back at the sound of it and when I got my bearings, I could see Norman sitting there missing the top half of his head. "Fuck me, that didn't go as planned, you're definitely dead now you awl fucker," I said as I stood there looking at what was left of Norman. I watched bits of Norman's skull and brains drip from the ceiling and I laughed as I said, "Not so smart now, sitting there with half your fucking head missing, are you?"

I made the decision that I should send a message with Norman and walked over to the table, as I stood there looking at the remaining 4 bullets, who would be next I thought, I said out loud, "Jonty, no you will keep for a while, Paul, no again, will look forward having you in my room, Sam definitely you would be last, as they say keep the best till last so unlucky for you Jason, you're next." I lifted his bullet and walked over to where Norman was sitting, I stood there with Jason's bullet in my hand wondering where to put it on Norman, then a saying came into my head, *Hear no evil, See no evil and Speak no evil,* so that's what it is then. I placed the bullet into what was left of Norman's right ear, the left ear was gone, in fact as I placed the bullet I think Norman's left ear fell onto the floor beside me. I shoved it right in there and stood back, it was showing a bit but there was no way I was hitting it with the hammer.

I unstrapped Norman from the chair and pulled him back into the wheel barrow, as I wheeled him out to my van I begin to think where was I going to dump his body. I pulled him out of the barrow and left him lying in the back of my van, I went back into my kill room and turned the light out, as I snapped the padlock shut I was still wondering where to leave Norman. I got into the van and started the drive back down towards the Shankill, driving down the Ballygomartin road, I looked at the clock on the dash board, it read 2.32 and I thought to myself, fuck me that was quick. I was still wondering, as I drove past Glencairn, where to dump Norman, as I got to the Woodvale park, I knew this was it so I pulled over just as the Woodvale met the Shankill. In fact, I wanted to leave a statement so I pulled Norman from my van, the road was dead, not a car light to be seen in any direction. I dragged his body over to the gates of Woodvale park and left him slouched up against them, I stood there just admiring my handy work and thought 1 down, 4 to go. I got back into my van and drove back up to my lock up and left the van round the back, got into my car and drove home.

On the way down the road, I put the radio on and I gave a smile as Madness was playing and *Welcome to the House of Fun* was on, I sang along only I changed the words to, 'Welcome to the house of pain' and I laughed as I sang the chorus.

I slept like a tap that night, in fact it was the best night's sleep I had had for a while.

CHAPTER 6

Detective Porter

As I woke the next morning, I had a real buzz at what I had just achieved and it was starting to eat away at me wondering who found Norman, so I decided to take a walk over to the shop just at the Woodvale Park. As I walked up Broom Street, I was getting excited at what I was going to find, as I turned onto the Shankill road I saw white tape across the road and a single policeman standing not letting any traffic or anyone past. I walked up to him. "What's going on Mr?" I asked.

The policeman looked at me, "There has been a murder," and he pointed down towards the gates of the Woodvale Park. I noticed a white tent that covered where I had left Norman.

"Who is it?" I asked, knowing rightly that it was Norman.

"I can't release that sort of information, so be on

your way."

I turned down Enfield Street and cut across one of the streets to try and get a better view, as I got to the end of the street again, it was taped and a peeler was standing there but this was a better view point. I could see 6 men in white boiler suits scouring the road and 2 other peelers standing talking, I noticed one of them, you couldn't miss him to be fair, he was about 6ft tall and of heavy build. I recognised him as the detective that came and interviewed me in the hospital when I had got kneecapped, Porter was his name and just at that he turned and looked over at me, for a brief moment we exchanged a glance and I thought to myself, catch me if you can Porter.

I turned and walked home, I smiled all the way back, I knew they had found the bullet and I thought to myself, let the games begin.

The word on the road spread fast and Billy rang me to tell me that it was Norman that had been killed and that an emergency committee meeting had been called for that night, so he needed me in for 5 o'clock.

I sat in all day just watching the TV waiting for any snip of news but it wasn't until 4pm that a news bulletin came on and there it was, the Shankill road, the tent just outside the Woodvale Park gates and the reporter said, "A local man in his 50s has been murdered and police are looking for anyone who seen or heard anything, no one has claimed responsibility but it is rumoured that the I.R.A are behind it."

That gave me an idea, if the I.R.A get the blame then I could continue playing the martyr and attend the funeral, it was perfect, not even Sam would suspect me so I could continue on planning my next target.

I got into work and the meeting was already taking place, Sam was effing and blinding looking for revenge and the rest of them were just adding fuel to the fire, it was perfect. As I walked towards the bar Billy said to me, "Alright Jonny, could you change a barrel for me? We are out of Harp." I walked into the store room and hung my coat up, as I turned round, Jonty was standing there I noticed a few bruise round his neck.

I just stood there waiting to see what he was going to do, he said, "I won't forget the other night ballbag and trust me, I will get you back."

I said to him, "I hope you don't forget 'cause I look forward to it, just me and you, in fact let's go now."

I took a step towards him and he put his hands up, "No Jonny, not here, not now but soon," and he turned and walked out, I don't know why but I wasn't scared anymore, in fact I loved the feeling of wanting to inflict pain and now with Norman still fresh in my mind, I wanted more. I changed the barrel and went back to the bar, I poured a few pints and brought them over to the table where Sam and his crew were busy planning, I looked at Jason who was about the same size as me and about the same weight, going round my head, I knew he would be easy to lift off the road but it was just a case of where and when.

I overheard Sam say, "Right its set, we lift one of them I.R.A bastards and nut them, in fact we lift 3, if they are going to target one of us then we kill 3, that should send a message to them." I couldn't believe what I was hearing I had started a war but it was a good cover for me.

I overheard Sam tell Jonty he was to do the murders within the next 3 days, they had to happen before Norman's funeral, he gave him a free run just whoever he could target as long as he got his body count, he would be happy.

I stood there dumb struck, Sam was a real evil man, he had just gave the go ahead for Jonty to kill probably 3 innocent Catholics and that disgusted me. I found myself standing in the middle of the bar just in my own silence, I couldn't hear a word being spoken, I just stood and stared at the 4 remaining men I knew I had to kill to end this and the focus I had was so real. Their faces were itched in my mind and it was that moment that I realised I had to do this soon.

I felt a hand on my shoulder. "Jonny are you ok?" I turned and Billy was standing there.

"Yes mate I am, what needs done?" I asked.

"Jonny you were miles away there son, is there anything bothering you?"

"No Billy, I'm ok, just day dreaming."

"Ok mate, can you finish off tonight? I have somewhere I need to be," Billy said.

"Yeah of course I can, you shoot off."

"Thanks Jonny, I will see you tomorrow about 6."

"Spot on Billy, see you then."

And with that Billy left, that just left me with Sam and the rest of them. I stood behind the bar and just watched and listened, it was about another half an hour or so and Sam stood up. "Right, it's set then, you know what to do." He then turned to me, "Jonny that's us done, you lock up after we leave, no one else is to come in tonight so you can have an early night."

I held my breath as each one of them finished their drinks and one by one walked out the door, I had a real bad feeling something was going to happen but it didn't and I gave a sigh of relief when the last one went. I walked straight over to the shutter and pulled it down, I pulled the bolt across on the inside to stop anyone else coming in and more importantly, to feel safe. As I cleaned up, I poured myself a pint and sat in front of the fire just in my own thoughts and flash backs of Gerrard came in to my head. I held my head in my hands and just tried my best to banish them, but I couldn't, I sat their shaking my head and I heard the squeals off Gerrard, I spun round in my chair to face the dance floor and I panicked. I could see myself and Gerrard sitting in the chairs in the middle of the floor and Jonty standing with the red hot poker, it scared the shit out of me and I spun back again, knocking my pint over and the glass broke as it hit the floor. The sounds and visions were gone, I stood up, my heart was beating like mad and I couldn't breathe, I gasped for air but a heaviness came over me and I passed out. When I came round, I was lying in a heap on the broken glass, I got myself together and got up, I had a small cut on my cheek but otherwise I was fine. I walked into the toilet to wash my face and as I threw some cold water over me, I looked in the mirror, I jumped back, I could see Norman's face in the mirror for a brief moment and then it was gone, I again threw some water over my face and just composed myself.

I walked back out into the bar and finished off cleaning the broken glass and mopping the floor, I lifted the shutter then turned the lights out, locked up and left.

I drove the short drive home and got into the sanctuary of my house, then I locked the front door and went up the stairs, I got undressed, got into bed and pulled the blankets up over my head and as I was exhausted, I went out like a light and didn't move until the next morning.

For the next couple of mornings, I started taking a drive round the Shankill looking for places to display my next kill and as I had the radio on, I heard a news bulletin come through that a Catholic taxi driver from Ardoyne had been shot and killed on the Antrim Road. I knew straight away it had to be Jonty and as I drove out onto the Crumlin Road, I drove straight into a police check point, as I pulled up I put my window down, the police man looked in and said, "Where are you going?"

I replied, "Just out for a drive, is there a problem with that?"

He opened the door and now very aggressively said, "Get out of the car you cheeky fucker."

"There is no need for that," I said as I undid my seat belt and got out, the peeler grabbed me and spun me round to face the side of the car, he kicked my legs apart as he called two other peelers over, he began to search me as he said to the other peelers, "Search the car and make sure you search it right."

I replied to him, "This is bang out of order, I haven't done anything."

He leant in and whispered in my ear, "Jonny Andrews I take it, and from Orkney Street who works in Heather Street social club."

"What the fuck are you on about, how do you know my name?"

"Shut up dickhead, just stand here and don't move."

I didn't know what the hell was going on but it was when one of the peelers came from behind the car carrying a package he handed to the peeler beside me when I heard him say, "And what's this we just found in your boot? I hope it's not what I think it is or you're in deep shit son."

"That's not mine, I have never seen that before, what the fuck is going on?" The peeler then grabbed my hand and put the package in it and then took it back.

"I think forensics will tell us different when they find your prints all over it," and he turned to one of the peelers and said, "Get transportation." Then he turned to me and said, "Jonny Andrews, we are arresting you on the suspicion of the distribution of drugs, your rights will be read to you at the station."

I turned and looked at the peelers know surrounding me and said, "Yous are a pack of black bastards, yous are setting me up and you know it," and at that, a police van pulled up and I was shoved inside.

On the drive to the police station, I couldn't believe what had went down and it worried me knowing my prints were now over that package, but it got me thinking that if they took my prints at the station they could link me to Norman's death if they found my van, or worse, my kill room.

It took what I thought was about 10 minutes and I heard gates being opened and then the van drove forward, stopped and turned its engine off. I knew I had arrived, the back doors where flung open and there standing in front of me was detective Porter he looked at me and said, "Nice to see you again Jonny, I have a proposition for you, can you come with me?"

I was dumb struck but I was ushered out of the van and was told to follow Porter into the building, as I looked round it struck me this wasn't a police station, it was just a single building but I followed him in to it and into a small room just inside the front door.

As I walked into the room, I saw it had a table and 2 chairs, detective Porter was already sitting down and on the middle of the table was the package that the peelers had planted on me. Porter said to me, "Sit down Jonny, would you like tea or coffee?"

I pulled the chair out, sat down and replied, "No I fucking don't want tea or coffee, I want to know what the fuck is going on."

"Calm down Jonny, you aren't in any trouble yet but I need you to listen to what I am going to tell you."

I sat there and just folded my arms. "Well let's hear it then."

"Now see this package I have hear," and he lifted the package, "there is enough drugs in this to send you down for a few years and with your prints all over it, we can tie you to it."

I replied instantly, "You know that's not mine, one of your fucking peelers planted it there and you know it."

I was furious but Porter replied, "Calm down Jonny, as I said you're not in any trouble if you co-operate."

"What do you mean co-operate?" I replied.

"Well that's what I want to speak to you about, you work in Heather Street and we know Sam and his crew operate out of there, we know you're not involved, we have done our homework, so my proposition to you is you be our ears and eyes on the inside and let us know if he is planning anything. As you have probably heard, a Catholic man has been shot dead and we know it's in retaliation for the death of one of Sam's men Norman, and we also know he won't stop there. But he is smart, any time we try to get him we can't get anything on him, so we need to either catch him with weapons or better still, trying to commit a murder which could see him being taken off the road for a very long time, what do you think Jonny?"

I didn't know what to say. "Can you give me some time to think about it? That's a lot you're asking of me, if Sam finds out I'm a dead man, so I am going to need time."

"We don't have time, Norman's funeral is Friday so that only gives us two days and my contacts tell me he wants 2 more Catholics dead before Norman goes into the ground, so it's important that you get close and find out when and where, we would protect you if anything went wrong."

"I will do it, what do I need to do?" I knew I couldn't let anyone else die at the hands of Jonty, I was the only one that was going to do the killing and I could use this to my advantage.

Detective Porter stood up, he reached into the inside pocket of his suit and pulled out a mobile phone, he handed it to me and said, "Ring me every morning at 9.30 on the dot, I will give you instructions, my number is on it and if you hear anything you ring me straight away. Listen out for times and places and what car they will be driving."

"If I do this, I need a clean slate, I would need to get out of Belfast, cause if you get Sam, his crew would do me in. I don't get on with them we have history so it is important that I get out."

"That's not a problem, we have safe houses as far as Scotland so we could give you a new life there."

"Right ok, I will do it." I had to agree with it as I needed to finish my plan and to be honest, I liked the thought of Porter not knowing I was the killer that was taking Sam and his crew down and that excited me, a new challenge now was that I could dangle the bodies in front of Porter and tease him with little clues.

As I shook hands with Porter, I knew I was probably signing my death warrant but it was a case of I get them before they get me. As we walked out into the yard, I saw my car parked and looked at Porter, he said to me, "We got your car drove up here so it wouldn't cause anyone asking questions if we dropped you off."

"Oh right," I replied, I had a feeling something

wasn't right, but I got into the car and drove out of the gates. I was in east Belfast, I recognised the road I was on when driving with Karen and it brought back memories of her, I missed her every day and just wish it could be different, but it was what it was and I was getting deeper and deeper involved in the dark side of Ulster.

I got home and as I had called for chips, I sat at the table and just thought about what I now had to do and to be honest, I wanted to get started.

CHAPTER 7

Hear No Evil

The next morning at 9.30, I phoned detective Porter, he answered straight away.

"Hello Jonny, have you anything for me?"

"No Porter, I don't, nobody was in last night, it was all quiet."

"Make sure you contact me straight away if you hear anything, my sources tell me that there is a hit planned for tonight and I need you to find out where, so tonight when you are in work, Sam will be there to organise it so I need to know straight away." Porter sounded in a panic, this was going down tonight and I was caught in the middle but I knew I if I got the chance to save some innocent Catholic, I had to do it.

After breakfast, I had a job to do now that the peelers had my prints, I had to clean my van and kill room, so off I went up Blackmountain. When I arrived, I thought about how I could make it more secure because if anyone had been there, how would I know? But as I parked my car round the back, I hit a pot hole and was bloody fuming as the tyre blew out. I got out of the car and walked round to the passenger side and, yep, bloody tyre ruined, so I hit it with a kick and this black box fell out from beneath the wing. I lifted it and looked at it, there was a green light flashing on it and the blood drained from me, it hit me that the peelers had planted this, it was similar looking to the one they had planted in the bar. I knew then that the peelers were keeping a close eye on my movements, I didn't know what to do, if I smashed it they would know I was on to them but if I left it they could track me to here, so I decided that I should plant it on another car and let them track it. The last thing I needed was the peelers showing up here and finding bits of Norman in my room.

I got my thoughts together and then started changing the wheel on my car, it took me about 30 minutes and to be honest, I had never changed a wheel before so it took me a while to figure out how to get the bloody thing off, but I got it changed. I had to leave the cleaning to another time as I needed to plant this bug on another car, I drove straight down home and parked outside my house, parked up a wee bit there was a *Ford Fiesta,* it was also white but just a bog standard 1.2l, it would do, so I casually walked over to it and bent down like I was tying my lace and slipped the bug into the inner guard. It must have been magnetised as it just stuck to the car like glue, I stood up and as I walked back down the street, I had a good look round to see if anyone had seen me but, all good, nobody was about. I walked into my house and made a cup of tea and a wee jam butty which reminded me off my ma and a Saturday morning heading out the door to meet Nigel.

I drove down to Larnick Way to get my tyre changed and it was bloody £32 quid for a new tyre. As I stood waiting, a guy in an awl clapped out car pulled in and got out, he walked over to where I was standing and said, "Here boy, I have some knock off gear in my car and it looks like it's about your size." He sounded like he was from down south, his accent was really strong, as he opened his boot I took a look inside it was like a bloody shop. As he opened up boxes, I could see he had as shit load of stuff from jeans, to shirts, to coats, he even had a couple of boxes of fireworks. As he lifted out a couple of pairs of jeans, I thought to myself, I'm not buying anything but when I looked at the jeans, they were class. They were *Levi's* and I knew in town you could pay anything up to 70 quid for them and he was only looking 15 quid a pop. I bought 3 pairs and a couple of shirts at a tenner a go, I also took a jacket of him which caught my eye, so all in all going down to get a new tyre cost me 130 quid, but it was a drop in the ocean as with my nanny's money, I still had the guts of 30 grand so a wee treat was good.

That night in the club, Porter was right, Sam and his crew were all there and they all went into the back room so I knew it was serious. I only got a chance to go in on a few occasions to bring drinks in and yep, they were talking about killing a Catholic. There were two new faces, both of them in their twenties, well built with shaven heads, they were tough looking boys and the talk was they were to do the hit, it was going to happen around 9pm and it was to take place over in East Belfast at a provisional I.R.A stronghold called Shortstrand. As I left the drinks on the table, I caught a glimpse of the keys of a car sitting on top of a bag that was in front of one of the killers, it had the logo of a *BMW* so I gathered that was the make of the car they were to use. I quickly went outside and took a look around and yep, an awl beat up red *BMW* was parked just down the street, I started panicking as I looked at my watch and it read 8.30pm, I knew I hadn't much time. I quickly rang Porter, when he answered I quickly said, "Red *BMW*, 9pm, Shortstrand." I immediately hung up and put the phone in my pocket and my timing couldn't have been any better as I turned to go back into the bar, the two killers came walking out with the bag. They walked straight past me and got into the BMW, I walked straight into the bar and continued to serve drinks. My nerves were wrecked, I hoped that Porter was able to get things in place to stop them murdering someone. I was glad it was two boys I didn't know cause if it had have been one of my targets, I couldn't have got it stopped as they would have been arrested, or worse, killed by the peelers and I definitely didn't want that to happen.

As I continued bringing drinks to the remaining men in the back room, they were sitting just listening to a police scanner waiting to hear about their target. But the longer the night went on, Sam was getting impatient and when the news came through that someone was shot dead in Shortstrand they all cheered, but as they listened on it was clear that it was one of Sam's men that had got shot and killed and the other one was arrested. Sam went berserk, he tipped the table over and threw a chair against the wall, that was my clue to get offside so I quickly went back into the bar and told Billy what was going on. Billy ran straight into the back room and I heard him shouting at Sam to calm down, one by one they came out and left in quite a hurry. Sam was the last one to leave and his fists were bleeding where it looked like he had punched the wall. He was still furious effing and blinding as he left the club. When Billy came out, he asked everyone to leave and we cleared up the mess that Sam had left, Billy said to me, "Sam is going nuts, I heard him saying he's planning to do another hit at the weekend and this time they won't miss."

"Fuck me Billy, what are we going to do? This is getting out of hand."

"I know Jonny, we will just keep our heads down and hopefully those Bastards get caught as well."

When I got home, I turned on the TV and as the news was just coming on, the headlines included, 'A man was killed and another arrested in a foiled murder attempt in East Belfast', the pictures were of the red *BMW* and a man lying on the road with a red blanket over him. I punched the air and was relieved at the outcome, so I decided then that it would a good time to execute Jason and I began to plan for the next night. I knew he was a creature of habit and that he always drank in the same bar down the road and then staggered up calling in for a kebab on the way. I knew the route he would take home and I had picked out a great spot to lift him.

The next morning, I went straight up to pick my van up. I gave it a quick clean out but had to through an awl blanket in it to cover the blood stains, I lifted the tools I needed and off I went to park the van in the bottom of Ainsworth Avenue, there were new houses being built so the street lights didn't work, it was perfect to pick Jason up.

It was my day off so I just took a dander round the *Co-op* to get a few messages then I called into Isabell's café on the road for lunch and it was bloody gorgeous, a fry up with extra bacon and a big mug of tea. If I was a cat I would have purred, I was really relaxed and was looking forward to later on.

I wandered up home and put my shopping away, I stuck the TV on and lit the fire. I lay down on the settee and watched some awl crappy film, but as I lay there, I fell asleep and it was only the sound of a taxi's horn that woke me. I jumped up, the fire had gone out so it was only the light of the TV that dimly lit the room, I looked at my watch and it was bloody 12.45am. "Fuck," I shouted as I knew Jason would be leaving the bar in about 15 minutes to go for his kebab. I threw on my coat and out the door I went, I took to my heels and ran to get to my van. When I arrived it just started raining so I opened it up and started the engine, I just let it tick over and then opened the side door and got inside. Just as I did when I got Norman, I waited and waited looking up the street but there was no sign of Jason, I looked at my watch it now read 1.30am. I was raging, I must of missed him, "Bastard," I said out loud and as I got out of the van I went to close the door and I heard a voice, as I turned to see who it was, the rain was now getting heavy.

"What the fuck are you doing here ballbag?" it was Jason and he was fully drunk, I didn't even answer him, I just buried my fist into his face. He fell straight back and hit his head off the road, he was out like a light, I grabbed him and trailed him into the back of my van where I cable tied his hands and feet. I didn't make the mistake this time by putting a rag in his mouth, I just left him lying there and slammed the door shut. I ran round and got into the van and sped off up to my kill room, it only took about 10 minutes and I arrived, I turned the van to get the side door as close to the door of my room. I turned the van off and just sat for a couple of minutes to catch my breath, my heart was beating so fast, but after a few minutes I got my breathing under control. I could hear Jason moaning and groaning so I knew he was still alive and that excited me, I got out in the bucketing rain and as I opened the door of my room and turned the light on, I could hear Jason kicking the door of my van. I lifted a baseball bat from just inside the door and then opened up the van, Jason kicked out at me but as he did he fell out of the van and onto the muddy ground, one good swing of the bat and a good crack across the coupon and Jason was unconscious again. I set the bat back in my room and grabbed him by the feet, I trailed him the short distance and lifted him into the chair then I cut the cable ties and strapped him in.

As he was coming round, I went outside and closed the van door. When I came in I heard him saying, "You're a dead man Jonny, when Jonty finds out about this, you're a fucking dead man."

I slowly closed the door and turned to face Jason, "Don't worry Jason, Jonty will have his turn but as for you, I have been waiting a long time for this moment, now let's have a bit of fun." I walked over and put the radio on, Cool Fm was on and a wee Bon Jovi number was playing. I sang along as I walked over to my bench to see what I was going to use first. "This Romeo is bleeding and you can't see his blood," I turned to Jason, "come on Jason sing along." He started screaming but I knew up here nobody could hear him, I walked over and turned the radio up a bit, Jason was now struggling to break free but he had no chance, he was well strapped to the steel chair. I lifted the heavy hammer and walked over in front of him, I smashed it down onto his left knee and crack, his knee cap shattered. I laughed as I smashed the other knee cap, Jason was screaming in pain, I just stood back and watched him in sheer agony, he was pleading with me to let him go but I just said to him, "This goes to the finish son, we have a bit to do yet." I walked over to my bench and lifted the garden shears, I had made sure when I was buying them that they were really sharp and to my amazement when I started cutting his fingers off, I couldn't believe how easy they came off. One by one they dropped onto the floor and as I cut each one, I sang him a wee nursery rhyme, "This little piggy went to market," *snip,* "This little piggy stayed at home," *snip.* Jason was squealing like an awl pig, which humoured me. "This little piggy had roast beef," *snip,* "aw fuck I got two that time, sorry Jason," and I laughed, "this little piggy got none," *snip.* I was now over to the other hand, "And this little piggy went squealing all the way home," *snip snip snip snip snip* and all of Jason's fingers and thumbs lay on the ground, the pain must have been too much as Jason passed out. The blood was pulsing out of what was left of his hands and I decided I didn't want him to bleed out so

I lifted the blow torch that I had and burnt the open wounds to stop the bleeding.

When Jason came back round, he was all over the place, his head rocked back and forward and he was just sobbing in pain. He tried to lift his head but he was done for, by the time I got the bleeding stopped, he had lost quite a lot of blood and was now barely conscious so I lifted my sheers again and as I removed his left ear, I said to him, "Hear No Evil Jason, I will keep this as a wee souvenir, I hope you don't mind." He passed out again, I walked over to my bench and left his ear down, I lifted one of the sharp knives and went back over to Jason, I lifted his chin and waited for him to open his eyes. I had the point of the knife in Jason's right ear and as he opened his eyes, I drove it into his brain, we exchanged a look for a brief moment and I could see his pupils dilate as he died, it was brilliant. As I stood there looking at him, I decided that Paul would be next so I lifted his bullet and walked back over to Jason. I was deciding where to put it and 'see no evil' came into my head so I got the knife out again and removed one of Jason's eyes, I was surprised how easy I got it out and I said to myself, "Jonny, if I didn't know any better you could have been a surgeon, you're quite handy with a knife," and I stood there laughing. I placed Paul's bullet in the socket and then went over and lifted the needle and thread and stitched the hole shut.

I got myself together, cut Jason free from the chair and trailed him through his own blood and out the door into the back of my van. The rain washed away any blood that was outside my room but when I slammed the van door shut and walked back into my room, I realised what a mess it was in and got back to thinking about Porter and if he ever traced me back to this place I would never see the light of day again and couldn't finish what I had started. I knew I had to get this place cleaned up and quick, so there would be no trace of what I was doing.

But my first thing I had to finish was where I was dumping Jason's body and with driving round all the streets of the Shankill, I had to make it look like the I.R.A had got him so I drove down the Woodvale Road and up to Workman's Avenue. The rain was starting to go off and the streets were empty, not even a car on the road, so I was good to go. I parked the van as close as I could get to the gates that separated the two communities and got out, as I walked round to open the side door I could hear the sound of a van and then I saw lights. My heart started racing, what if it was the peelers? I ran round to the driver's side and got in, I was about to start the engine when I saw in my passenger side mirror that it was the bloody milk man and I gave a sigh of relief as he just drove by and didn't even take me under his notice. I got out and walked back round, I waited a few seconds before I opened the sliding door, it was so quiet I slid the door open and trailed Jason out by the feet. He fell out of the van and cracked his head on the pavement, I said, "Oh dear, that's gonna leave a mark," and laughed as I trailed him over to the gates. I propped his body up against the gates and placed what was left of his hands over his ears but they wouldn't stay, his arms kept falling down so I walked over to my van and lifted a couple of cable ties. I joined them together and as I walked back over to Jason, I lifted one of his hands and placed it on the side of his head. I wedged my knee against it as I lifted the other hand and placed it on the other side of his head, I got the cable tie and wrapped it round his head and hands, keeping them in place and perfect. It was exactly how I wanted to leave him, Porter will love it, it would definitely give him something to think about.

As I drove back up to leave the van off, I was well proud of my masterpiece and looked forward to see what the media and especially Porter, would have to say.

CHAPTER 8

Porter And The Deal

I couldn't sleep all night, I could just see Jason sitting slouched up against the peace gates and the morning couldn't have come quick enough. I didn't even take breakfast, I just wanted to see what was happening up at Workman's Avenue so I drove down Ainsworth Avenue and parked just at the top of Duvary Parade then walked the short distance to Workman's Avenue. As expected, a few people had gathered and the police tape was across the road, as I walked over I asked some man standing, "What's happened mate?"

He looked at me and replied, "They have found a body right up against the gates and he was in a mess, the word is he is missing his fingers, some dirty fucker has tortured him. The forensics are on the scene looking for any clues so the whole street and part of the Springfield Road is closed off. I can't even get back into my house to get a fucking cup of tea," he was really angry when he said that but inside I was really happy and had to hide my excitement so I just replied, "That's hectic mate, do you know who it is?"

"They think it's one of Sam's crew from down the road," he replied.

"Oh right, that's going to cause trouble, if it is, big Sam will crack."

"Crack, crack? Are you having a laugh? He will go berserk, fuck knows what he will do now, this will be two of his crew that the I.R.A has killed. He will definitely go on a revenge attack now, there will be no-one safe, he will just want blood."

"Is that who they think killed him?"

"Don't know but it has to be them, who else could it be?"

I smiled and said, "Aye you're probably right," and I walked off. Just at that, the phone that Porter gave me rang, I lifted it out of my pocket and answered it. "Hello, who's this?" I said sarcastically.

"Hello, hello, who do you think you're talking to? I think you forget you work for me."

"Sorry detective, I am only messing with you." As I walked back down Duvary Parade, I was so chuffed with myself. "How can I help you this fine morning?"

"Help me, fucking help me? Have you not heard that one of Sam's crew has been executed?"

"No I haven't, I am just about to get breakfast, who was it?"

"Jason, one of his right hand men, he will go nuts and that is why you need to be in work tonight to find out any information 'cause I know he will want revenge."

Porter was going nuts and that pleased me, the thought of him not knowing he was talking to the killer excited me and I thought I would test his knowledge a bit further.

"I have been thinking detective, this information you require must be worth a bit."

Porter spoke up, "You listen here Jonny, you work for me and it's only me that is keeping you out of jail so you think long and hard about what you're going to say next."

"Well to be honest, that's two of Sam's crew dead now and I would probably be safer in jail so pick me up any time, I have nothing to lose," and at that I hung the phone up.

As I got into my car, the phone rang again, I let it ring for about 10 seconds and then answered, "Hello Isabel's café, can I have your order please?" I laughed as I said that.

"Don't get fucking funny with me Jonny, now listen son, I need that information, I need you to meet me later, about 3pm. I will meet you at the Park Avenue Hotel off the Hollywood Road over in East Belfast, the bottom car park, make sure you're there," then he hung up.

I drove down to Isabel's café and went in for a fry up, I sat there planning out my day and I knew I had to go up to my kill room and clean it up. So after I finished my breakfast, I drove down to the *Co-op* and bought 4 big bottles of bleach and 4 big towels. I drove straight up to my room and began to get it cleaned up, I decided to light the fire to burn any of the evidence (Jason's fingers).

I poured the bleach on raw and got a big yard brush that I had bought earlier in the week and began to brush the blood out the door. It took me about an hour to get it all cleaned up and I burnt the towels and the 3 empty bottles of bleach as well.

I still had one bottle left and I thought to myself, how sore would it be if you drank this stuff? So I left that in the back of my head and thought maybe I'll give Paul a wee bleach cocktail to sample.

Time was ticking by as I knew I had the meeting with Porter and also I had to get my van cleaned up, but that would have to wait until tomorrow.

I drove back down home and made some lunch, as I sat with a mug of tea and a ham sandwich Karen came into my head, it was probably the thought of going over to the Park Avenue Hotel that sparked it. it reminded me of the night that her mum and dad treated us to dinner when we got engaged, it saddened me at losing her but knew it couldn't be any other way. If I could have turned back time, we should have run off together and started a new life somewhere else, but I knew it was too late for that now.

I threw my cup and plate into the half-filled sink of dishes and as I walked back through my living room, I stood and took a good look round. It was bloody stinking, dirty clothes hung over the chair in the corner, the carpet hadn't been vacuumed in weeks and the window was filthy too. I thought to myself, if my ma could see her house now, she would turn in her grave, so I gathered all the dirty clothes up and put them in a bin bag. I walked out and put them in the boot of my car then walked back inside the house and tided up a bit, but I didn't have time to give it a good clean as it was now 2.40pm and I knew I had to go.

I drove down the Shankill and called into the dry cleaners and left my dirty clothes, the girl behind the counter asked, "Do you want these ironed as well for an extra two quid?"

I replied to her, "That would be great, can I pick them up in a couple of days?"

"Yes that would be fine," and she gave me a docket.

I got into my car and drove over to meet Porter, I arrived dead on 3pm and parked facing the only entrance. No other car was in the car park so I just sat and listened to the radio, the news had just came on and I listened intently to the girl speaking and YES, the girl said, "A body has been found at the bottom of Workman's Avenue in west Belfast, the police have put a cordon up securing the area, a male in his twenties has been found tied up against the gates separating the two communities. Police have issued a statement saying that it is being connected to a previous killing of another member of the U.F.F and that they believe it is the same killer and are asking if anyone has any information regarding this murder to contact police at Tennent Street or on the free phone number."

"Yes," I said, as I banged my fist on the steering wheel, I was hoping they would connect the murders and I said to myself, let the games begin.

Just at that, a car pulled into the car park and

pulled alongside my car, it was Porter. He put his window down as I did and he said, "Get in Jonny, we have a lot to discuss." At that, I got out of my car and got into his, as I closed the door he turned his engine off.

"Jonny this body that we found was in a real mess, we are keeping the details away from the general public but my concern is that Sam will want revenge once he finds out what someone has done to one of his own. There will be blood and I mean, not one life, he will want something big, so I need you to be alert as he will want to react before his man's funeral."

"When you said the body was in a mess, what was done to it?"

"I can't divulge that information, all I can tell is we are dealing with a serial killer and that he took his time with him but there is something bothering me about it."

"What is it?" I was really egger to find out what he knew.

"Whoever is doing this isn't going to stop, he has already told us who is going to be next but to be honest, I am more concerned about what Sam is going to do 'cause he could bring this country back into war again and a lot of people will die."

"What do you mean, the killer has phoned you and told who he is going to target next?"

"No Jonny but we found something on the body that was similar to what we found on Norman's body, so that connects the two and we fear that another of Sam's crew is next."

"Oh my God, what are you going to do? Are you going to warn him he is next? Is it me? Is that why you wanted to talk to me to tell me?" I knew it wasn't but I needed Porter to think I was on his side.

"No Jonny it isn't you, I need you to stop more innocent people getting killed, you are the only one they trust so we really need you to get the information from Sam."

"But what if Sam finds out I am working for you? It's too risky, I would rather go to jail, I know what Sam is capable of," I paused and then said, "So if I am going to do this I will need enough money to start a new life somewhere else."

"I understand that Jonny, that's why I am here, if you help bring Sam and his crew down we will make sure that you are moved to Scotland and we would put 20 grand in a bank account for you to start a new life, you would have a new identity as well, a clean slate, do you understand that Jonny?"

"Yes I understand, but 20 grand won't last long, I would need a job as well."

"We can sort that out as well, so do we have a deal?" and at that we shook hands and I got out of Porter's car who drove off immediately.

I got into my car with a big smile, I thought to myself, he knew nothing, he hadn't a clue that it was me and I was chuffed to bits he called me a serial killer, a professional killer, me, wee Jonny from the road. Or did he know it was me and wanted me to take them out I wondered, would he still pay me the 20 grand when they are all dead? I laughed.

I drove out of the Park Avenue Hotel and onto

the Hollywood Road, I turned down towards the Newtownards Road and headed for home. As I got to just about the bottom of the Hollywood Road, I spotted Karen coming from work, my heart missed a beat. Half of me wanted her to see me but the other half was scared she would, so I slouched down in my seat and just carried on driving by. She hadn't noticed but god, I missed her, I promised myself that when this was finished I would ring her and arrange to meet her, I still loved her and wanted this over.

Later that night in work it was just Sam and about 20 other men, they were all sitting round four tables that were put together and Billy's face said it all. I knew by looking at him that Sam was planning something big and then I heard one of the men saying, "It's settled then, we go on Saturday morning 10am, Sinn Fein Headquarters and we go in hard, Adams is the target but whoever is there is to be taken out as well, the more the merrier."

I didn't recognise all of them but I was focused on one face, Paul and I had already in my head what I wanted for him so I was in two minds, should I phone Porter and give him the target or just concentrate on keeping Paul alive until I get to him.

As I stood behind the bar pouring pints, Billy came over, "Are you ok Jonny you seem quiet tonight?"

"Aye Billy I'm fine, just don't like being in the same room as these ones."

"Aye I know how you feel Jonny, I am more fearful of when they carry out this attack that the I.R.A will target here son and we get caught up in it."

"Billy we are already caught up in it, we know when and where they are going to attack, so I don't know about you but I hope they get caught and jailed."

"Aye Jonny that would be the best outcome, get them off the streets and get the road back to normal but don't let anyone hear you talk like that 'cause at the minute everyone is trigger happy, especially with this serial killer on the loose."

"Serial killer, Billy, are you serious? That sounds like something that goes on in Downtown New York, not in bloody Belfast and definitely not the Shankill."

"I know Jonny, it sounds like something out of *Crimewatch* but it's happening, so be very careful, especially when you are going home at night, the talk is that the killer is lifting them off the street and torturing them."

"I will Billy, don't worry about me, I'm too smart for that, we need to worry about this lot," and at that I looked round to where the men were sitting and they all stood up and started leaving the club. Sam was last to leave and I was really worried, if he had of been effing and blinding it would have been easier to understand but he was as cool as a cucumber, a real ice look about him, which frightened me.

He said to Billy, "We will send a message out this time, I want you to get a group on for Saturday night and make sure you get caterers in as well, we are going to celebrate on Saturday night."

"Ok Sam, leave it with me, I will sort it," and at that Sam left.

Billy turned to me, "You will need to be here on

Saturday night Jonny, can you be in for 3pm son? It's not going to be an easy night, especially if they succeed in what they are going to do."

"Aye Billy, I will be here," and at that Billy let me go on home.

All night I pondered what I should do, phone Porter and tell him about the hit on the Falls Road and get it foiled, but then it would mean Paul and Jonty would be caught if not killed, or just say nothing and let it happen? it was a real dilemma and the thought of having someone's life in my hands really worried me, but the thought of losing out on seeing Paul and especially Jonty and the look on their face when they knew it was me going to kill them was more important, so let it happen was my decision.

Norman's funeral passed off peacefully which was a huge relief to everyone, I think none of the U.F.F wanted to get arrested, especially Sam and his hit squad, they all had Saturday to do and that's why I think it was a private funeral, family and close friends only.

It was now Friday and time was ticking by too quick, I had decided that if Sam's hit was a success that I would take Paul after the do on Saturday night. I got everything put in place and as Paul was from Shankill estate, that on the way down from the club, I would lift him right off the Shankill Road so I parked my van right outside the doctor's surgery late on Friday afternoon and walked back up to work. The Shankill had a real bad atmosphere about it, everyone I met on the way back up talked about the same thing (the serial killer and if he would strike again).

When I arrived at Heather Street, I noticed a black car sitting down the street a bit, I had never seen this car before and as I looked closer, two men were sitting in it then the window of the driver's side started going down, the man poked his head out. "Jonny, come here a minute."

I looked at him, my heart was racing but I walked over, when I could see right into the car I noticed the two of them where wearing suits and when the man in the passenger side spoke up, I knew it was Porter. "Jonny you have to get the information, we have been informed that a hit is going to happen tomorrow morning but we still don't know where and that's your job to find out."

"Fuck me Porter, are you determined to get me killed? What the fuck are you doing here, right here outside the club? Could you not have phoned me? What if anyone sees, I'm a fucking dead man," I replied.

"Calm down Jonny, I just need you to understand that this is going down and you are the only one to stop it."

And at that the window went up and they drove away.

I stood there not knowing what to do, I just looked around to make sure nobody had seen and I walked into the club.

Billy had already bottled up and a few punters were already in drinking, I walked into the toilet to have a piss and as I washed my hands, I broke out in a cold sweat. I got some cold water and threw it over my face, as I looked in the mirror, a faded face looked back, I looked hard and I jumped back in shock, it was Jason looking back at me. I closed my eyes and held them shut tight, I was breathing really fast, my heart was thumping, I opened my eyes and he was gone. "Fuck me," I said, "these flash backs are getting worse." I dried my face and went back out in to the bar, Billy was serving drinks and he looked at me he said, "Jonny are you ok? You look like you have seen a ghost."

"Yeah Billy, I'm fine, just tired mate," and at that I walked behind the bar and started serving the next punter, as the night went on we got really busy and it was about 10 o'clock when Orange Lil came in. I was surprised as she hadn't been in absolute ages and she was back to her old ways, short skirt and low cut top with no bra, she sat in her usual seat and I could feel her eyes burn through me, she waited her turn to be served and then she said, "Hello good looking, how have you been?"

"Yeah I'm ok Lilly, where is Victor?"

"Have you not heard? We aren't together anymore, I live just off Conway Street, just me and the child."

"Oh right Lilly, what did you have?"

"A wee boy, he is the spit of his da."

"Aw that's lovely, who has him tonight?"

"Oh his da has him, he takes him on a Friday and brings him back Sunday afternoon, it's great, means I can go out on the drink."

"Very good, what would you like to drink, the usual?"

"Yes sexy, make it a double, here I've been thinking…"

"Careful Lilly, that's dangerous you thinking," and I laughed.

"Hey you, I will slap the jaws off you, less of your cheek," and Lilly laughed as well.

"But seriously Jonny, now that I am single and Victor has the child every weekend, my house is free if you ever fancy a coffee call in, Saturday afternoons are free for you aren't they?"

I stood there, my face going a bit red. "Aye they are Lilly, but seriously Lilly are you asking me what I think you're asking?"

She sat their smiling, "Yes Jonny, that's exactly what I am asking, would you be interested?"

"You're a nightmare Lilly."

"I could be your Saturday afternoon thing if you want," she said, now taking a big drink of her double vodka and diet *Coke*.

"You never know your luck Lilly, maybe take you up on that," I said laughing, I thought to myself no chance but it kept her thinking.

After we got the last punter out, Billy said to me, "Jonny I need you here tomorrow for 5pm, don't be late cause if Sam has his way then it's going to be a rough night, they will all be here and probably all get blitzed, we need to let the band in and the caterer as well."

"Ok Billy I'll be here." I knew I had everything planned and set up for Paul and the closer it was getting, the more excited I was, I walked back up home and I was like a child waiting for Christmas. I had tea and toast and went straight to bed.

CHAPTER 9

50 Shades Of Black And Blue

The next morning, I woke about 10am and was wondering if Sam had been successful in his murder attempt on the Falls Road. I turned the TV on to see if there was any news but there was nothing. I made some cornflakes and sat at the table, I had just finished when a news bulletin came on and yes, he had, two men were killed and another two critically injured in a shooting at the headquarters of Sinn Fein on the Falls Road. It was reported that two men both wearing balaclavas entered the building just before 10am and opened fire indiscriminately with automatic weapons killing two men instantly and injuring two other men who are fighting for their lives in the Royal Victoria hospital, the assailants are of medium build, about 5ft 10 inches tall and escaped in a dark coloured car heading towards the city centre. Police are asking anyone who was in the area at the time to report anything that they saw to the police on the free phone number and at that, a telephone number came across the TV screen.

Oh my god, I thought, *he has really done this*, my blood ran cold and I knew Sam would be chuffed to bits knowing he had killed 2 men and critically injured another 2 The thoughts of Billy came to mind and what we had talked about, that the I.R.A would strike back, but then that would be my cover to kill Paul.

I went back upstairs and got washed and changed, I had to go down the Shankill to do a bit of shopping as I had no grub left in the cupboard, so off I went to the *Co-op*. As I got to the second aisle, who was there? Bloody Orange Lil again not wearing much clothes, as I walked up towards her she bent down to get something from the bottom shelf and yep, just the usual not wearing a bra, her boobs near fell out. I said to her, "Easy there Lil, you're going to give yourself and injury."

She looked up, "Aw Jonny, I would recognise that sexy wee voice anywhere, are you stalking me?"

"You wish Lil."

"I do Jonny, do you fancy that wee cup of coffee?" and she winked at me.

"Aye why not Lil."

I thought I would call her bluff but she coughed as she replied, "Brilliant, let's go now, just leave your messages on this shelf and you can come back for them after I am done with you."

I looked at my watch which read 12.30 and I thought to myself why not? I put my messages down, she did as well and we walked out of the shop and the short distance round the corner to her house, as she put the key in the door she turned to me and said, "Now Jonny this is our wee secret, nobody needs to know."

"I know Lil, I'm not that bloody stupid," and I walked in through the front door, she closed the door behind me and ushered me up the stairs. As I walked into her bedroom, she was getting undressed behind me, I felt her top hit me on the back of the head I turned to see her just wearing the skimpiest of knickers, well they weren't that skimpy they probably were about a size 20 but the size of her arse just swallowed them up. She started undressing me, first my top which when she was talking it off got stuck on my ears but she gave it a good tug nearly pulling my ears off with it. "Fuck sake Lil, easy on."

"Easy on Jonny, I have been waiting a long time to have you here."

She then un- buttoned my jeans and dropped them to the floor, she pushed me back onto the bed where she removed my shoes and socks and then she slowly removed my boxers. She said to me, "How do you feel Jonny are you horny?"

"Yes Lil fir fuck sake just get over here."

"Not yet Jonny." She walked over to a set of drawers at the side of her bed, she brought out four ties then came back over and tied one of them round one of my wrists.

I said to her, "What are you doing Lil?"

She replied, "Just go with it Jonny, you will love it."

I thought why not I would try anything once, she tied both my wrists to the headboard and both my ankles to the bottom of the bed. I was lying their completely at her mercy and she loved it, she started kissing my feet then my legs, up she kept going, my thighs then my hips. She was now straddling me and fuck she was heavy, I could hardly breath, as she sat on me she took the bobble out of her tied back hair she shook her head. I think she thought she looked like one of the girls out of *Baywatch* but from my view she looked like someone off *Crimewatch*, she started rubbing her hair on my chest then across my face, it was bloody stinking, it smelt like she hadn't washed it in weeks and to make it worse one of the bloody hairs got in my mouth. I coughed and started choking on it, she put her finger in my mouth and fished it out, tears were traveling down my cheeks and it was then I knew I had made a mistake, she leant down and lifted something from beneath the pillow it was another piece of cloth, this time she placed it over my eyes and tied it behind my head, I couldn't see a thing.

I said, "Lil I don't like this, can you untie me?"

"Oh not yet Jonny, I am only getting started."

"Fuck sake Lil, I will have sex with you just untie me."

She hit me a slap in the face.

"You're my bitch now Jonny and I'm going to have my fun with you."

At that she got off me and said, "Now Jonny I'm not going to hurt you they say it heightens your senses now just lie back and enjoy this."

I didn't know what to say, I was stuck, I couldn't do

anything else but just lie there on her bed in her house and with Lil now going through the drawers at the side of her bed, I didn't know what to expect. I was sweating, the fear of being stuck here and not knowing what was going to happen frightened me, I should have taken Billy's advice and have avoided Orange Lil like the plague. I heard the drawer close and thought here goes nothing and *crack,* she hit me with what I thought was a piece of rope and it stung like a wasp sting right across my thighs and then I heard her crack it again and I realised it was a fucking whip.

"How do you like that Jonny?"

"It's fucking sore Lil."

And *crack*, she whipped me across the chest. "Just take it Jonny take it like a man," she said as she whipped me about another 10 times, she really whipped me good and she was laughing and saying, "Yes Jonny, do you like it bitch?" I was stinging all over my legs, my arms, my chest, she even hit me across the balls which when she did I gave a yelp as my dick and balls where aching.

"Fuck sake Lil that's enough of that, it's bloody sore."

"Oh I agree Jonny." As she again opened up her drawer, I didn't know what to do but when I heard a buzzing sound, I got frightened. I tried to break free from my clasps but it was all in vain. Lil said, "Now, now Jonny, take it easy, you're going to enjoy this."

She put something on my feet, it tickled and I thought that's better than the whip, I relaxed as she started moving it up my body, my calves, my knees then my thighs. She went past my dick and she began rubbing my nipples with it, then round my lips, she told me to open my mouth and I stupidly did. She put this thing in my mouth and it was now vibrating that hard I thought my teeth were going to fall out, I gagged as she put it too far in and she removed it.

"Fuck sake Lil, I couldn't breathe there."

"Then hold your breath for this then Jonny."

She shoved the fucking thing up my arse and I squealed as she forced it right up there, it felt about six feet long and I thought at one stage it was going to come out my mouth. I was in sheer agony and when she pulled it out, tears were traveling down my cheeks, she removed the blind fold from me and she just stood at the bottom of the bed silent, it scared me.

I said to her, "Can you untie me Lil I need to be somewhere?"

She just stood there silent rocking from side to side, I was starting to get annoyed but she didn't answer, I was pleading with her but got no reaction.

I kept saying, "Lil are you listening to me? I have to get to work, Billy will be furious if I'm late."

She starting getting dressed and then turned to me and said, "Don't you be going anywhere Jonny boy I am starving now and I am going to get a fish supper, I will be back shortly for round two."

At that she walked out the door, I shouted after her, "Fuck sake Lil you can't leave me here like this."

She walked back in again and said, "Oh yes I can Jonny, you are going to be here for a while just relax and I will see you soon."

She walked out and closed the door behind her.

As I lay there I said to myself, *Fuck sake Jonny, you can do it the best, now what the hell are you going to do? This psycho bitch is going to keep you here as her sex toy.* My mind was racing, I had to be in work, I had to make sure I got Paul tonight but I was trapped like a rat. For about 5 minutes I just lay there wondering what to do and there was only one thing for it, I was going to have to bust the bed apart to break free. I pulled and pulled at the headboard, it started to get loose and with one big pull it came away from the bed, it bloody hit me a smack in the head but I could now sit up. I reached the headboard over my head and put my knees up against it and broke it in half, I used one bit of it to smack the bottom of the bed and it came away as well, as I broke free the bed fell to bits round me. I untied the ties that Lil had used, I was free, I quickly put my clothes back on and got out of there as quick as I could and not a minute too soon as I got out the front door I could see Lil walking down the street. I quickly walked the opposite way and round the corner and headed for home to get cleaned up.

When I got in it was now 3pm, bloody nearly 2 hours she had me in that house, but I think I had a lucky escape when I took my top off to get changed for work, the welts all over my chest were bloody aching. I took my jeans off and my legs were the same, I walked back down to the kitchen and put the kettle on, I lifted a basin out and the bottle of *Dettol* that my ma always swore by and put some in the basin. I filled it up with hot water and soaked a tea towel in it, as I cleaned the welts, they stung like hell but I counted my lucky stars as I could have still been at the mercy of Orange Lil.

CHAPTER 10

Bump And Run

On the way down to work, I was walking like John Wayne, my arse was bloody sore and my chest and legs were smarting but I knew I had a job to do and was really looking forward to it.

I got there about 4.30pm and Billy had already opened up, there was a few punters in and I was glad that Orange Lil wasn't there, as I walked behind the bar Billy said to me, "What's up with you hop along?"

"Billy you have no idea, you wouldn't believe me even if I did tell you."

"Oh now Jonny spill the beans, that sounds interesting."

"Fuck no Billy, I want to forget about it you just need to know I will be staying away from Orange Lil from now on."

At that Billy laughed his head off. "Well I did warn

you, you friggen muppet, tell me you didn't."

"Didn't even get the chance Billy but I really don't want to talk about it."

If I did tell Billy, he would of slagged the life out of me for months, so I just decided that I would put it to the back of my mind and try and forget about it.

The front door opened and a girl with blonde hair came in, I had to look twice, at first I thought it was Karen but as she walked in she said, "Is one of you's Billy?"

Billy spoke up, "Yes I'm Billy, how can I help you?"

"I'm Jennifer, I am here to do the catering for tonight."

"Oh right love, Jonny here will give you a hand with whatever you need done."

At that I said, "Hi, what do you need?"

Jennifer replied, "My van is outside, I would need a hand with the trays but could you set me a couple of tables up in the corner first?"

Jennifer handed me a bag.

"Here is some table cloths, if you can put them on I will start bringing the food in."

"Yeah no worries," and at that I pushed two tables together over in the corner and put the table cloths on, I then followed Jennifer outside and started to bring trays of sandwiches in. As we were outside, I nearly dropped a whole tray of sausage rolls, I said to Jennifer who nearly had a buckle in her eye, "O shit they nearly went there," as I juggled the tray to stop them falling.

Jennifer said to me, "Jesus Jonny be careful, I only have enough of them for a hundred people."

"No worries Jennifer I caught them, here that's not a Belfast accent, where are you from?"

"I'm from Newtownards, I have lived there all my life, I take it you from the road Jonny?"

"Aye all my days, I know a fella from Ards I used to work for him on a Saturday, he is a lemonade man would you know him? His name is Nigel, I think his wife is called Dorothy."

"You are joking me Jonny, that's my mum and dad."

"Fuck off no its not."

"Yeah it is, my dad is Nigel the Maine man, he does the lemonade up here."

"Holy shit it's a small world, how is Nigel doing I haven't seen him in ages?"

"Yeah he's doing alright still working away."

"That's brilliant, tell him I was asking about him."

"Will do Jonny."

And at that we carried the rest of the food in, just as the group was arriving, I got lumbered into carrying the bloody speakers in and when I lifted them my chest smarted like hell so I was glad to get behind the bar and serving drinks.

It was now 6pm and the bar was filling up but no sign of Sam and the rest of his crew, they didn't way in until about half seven and when they did a huge cheer went up. They were treated like bloody heroes, they didn't even put their hand in their pocket for a drink, when the band started playing at 8pm the place was bouncing. It was a sash bash with all the loyalist tunes playing, everyone was singing and dancing but I was focused on one person, Paul and to be honest when someone offered to buy him a drink, I made sure I gave him a double. I wanted him blitzed out of his head so it would be a gift to get him in the back of my van.

The food was served around 9 and when the band started playing again about 9.45, I gave Jennifer a hand to put her trays back into her van. She said she would stay on but I told her that it would probably end in a row tonight, she would be better off to head home to Ards and she left.

I returned into the bar where Billy asked me to change a barrel, as I was in the back store changing the barrel I noticed a length of hose pipe and I had an idea that I could use it later, so I rolled it up and put it into my coat pocket. I returned out to the bar and went back behind to serve drinks, the crowd were bouncing when penny arcade came on, Billy and me were snowed under behind the bar we never got a minutes break not even to go for a piss but it put the night in quickly. About 12.30am, Billy rang the bell for last orders and I never seen as much drink drunk inside half an hour in my life, everyone were ordering doubles and by 1.15am the only ones left were Sam and his crew so game on.

Billy said to me, "Jonny it's been a long night if you want to head on I will lock up tonight, I'm sure these ones won't be much longer anyway, we will come in an hour early tomorrow and clean up as I am knackered as well."

"No worries Billy, thanks mate, in for 4 then tomorrow?"

"Yeah Jonny that's perfect, sure I will see you then."

As I walked into the store and got my coat, when I walked back through the bar, Paul was all over the place he was really drunk and I thought to myself, see you soon son.

When I got outside it was raining so I put my hood up and started walking down the road to get to my van, I knew Paul would be about 15 minutes behind me so I was in no rush.

My van was still where I left it so I opened it up and sat in the driver's seat, I just sat and watched as the odd car drove past but on a night like this, nobody was out walking so it was quiet just the sound of the rain beating of my van roof. I waited about 10 minutes then got out and opened the side door, I looked up the Shankill and noticed in the distance a loan figure staggering towards me, I couldn't really see him as the rain was getting heavy but I guessed it was Paul so I got myself together. I was really focused I knew what I needed to do, I sat directly opposite the sliding door of my van on a wee wall with my hood up and a baseball bat tucked in tight to my left leg so Paul couldn't see it when he walked down. I glanced up the road and it was Paul, he wasn't wearing a coat and he was like a drowned rat, he was now about 20 feet away staggering from side to side, he didn't even notice me sitting there, to be honest I don't think he could see 2 feet in front of himself. But he was now 10 feet away, then 5 feet and as I stood up in front of him, my head still bent down so I could just see him out of my hood he stopped and said, "What the fuck?"

I lifted my head and said, "Hello Paul, it's time," and at that I swung my baseball bat and near took his head off, he fell to the ground and was out cold, I threw my bat into the van and dragged him inside. I went through the same routine and cable tied his hands and feet, I slammed the door shut and had a quick look round to make sure nobody had seen, all clear, I got into the driver's seat and put the keys in the ignition. As I went to start the engine it just turned over really slow and then *click click click* and then nothing, my heart started beating faster and faster, I tried it again but nothing then I noticed the bloody sidelights had been left on. I then realised the battery was flat "Shit, shit," I said as I thumped the steering wheel, what was I to do? I had Paul unconscious lying in the back and no way of getting him to my kill room, my heart was thumping uncontrollably as I noticed a car pull up behind me, when I looked in my side view mirror I saw a policeman get out of the car, he was walking towards my van (oh my God, I thought, I'm caught). I wound down my window just as the peeler got up alongside it.

"Hello sir what seems to be the problem?"

"My van won't start, I think it's the battery."

"Aw that's easy to fix sir, we will give you a bit of a push, do you know how to bump start it?"

"No I don't," I replied.

"Oh right then, you and my colleague will push it and I will get it going for you."

Holy shit, I thought, *if Paul comes round I am screwed.*

So I agreed and got out of the van and walked to the back of it with the peeler who went and explained to his mate what was happening,

The other peeler and me got at the back of the van and waited for the first peeler to give us a shout, which he did and off we went starting pushing, we got about 15 feet down the road when the van jerked and started the peeler revving the life out of it. It had started, he stopped the van and got out leaving it ticking over, I was dumb struck, I just stood there in the pissing rain not believing at what had just happened.

"Thank you so much, you're a real life saver," I said.

"Not a problem sir, all in a day's work," and at that the two peelers got into their car and drove off.

I waved them off and got into my van and just in time too, when I turned my van to go up the Shankill, I heard Paul moaning in the back. I laughed to myself and turned the radio on to drown out his cries.

It took me about 10 minutes but I had arrived, I turned the van and opened the big heavy door, I went inside and turned the light on, I took a deep breath and said, "Well here we go."

I walked over to the van and opened the sliding door, Paul kicked out but I knew he would. I just stood back and laughed as he lay there effing and blinding, shouting at me that he was going to kill me.

I answered back, "Now now Paul, I think you will find I will be doing the killing, now let's get you out of that van and into a nice wee comfortable seat."

I grabbed his feet and started pulling him forward,

he was struggling like a rabbit caught in a snare so when he hit the ground, he did his best to try and crawl under the van. I grabbed his feet again and just trailed him face down into the room, I left him lying in the middle of the floor and went outside and closed the van door, I checked I hadn't left the lights on and walked back into the room. Paul was squealing and shouting but I slowly closed the big door behind me, as I watched him rolling round the floor I stood there just watching him squirm and then lifted my bat. I walked over slowly and he did his best to try and keep me away, kicking out, but one swift thump across the head and he was out. I dropped the bat and lifted him up onto the chair, I went and lifted a knife from my bench and cut the cable ties, I strapped him in and just waited for him to come back round.

When he did, I was waiting, standing in front of him with my heavy hammer.

"Wakey wakey Paul, back with the living." He lifted his head and as he was now looking me straight in the eye, I came down with the hammer right across his right knee and wow, what a sound as I heard bones break, Paul screamed out in agony and whack, the left knee smashed as well. Paul passed out again which give me time to strap his head back and in a fixed position, I went to my coat and lifted out the length of hose and went to my bench and lifted the bottle of bleach, when Paul came back from the dead, I told him to open his mouth but he refused.

I said to him, "We can do this the hard way or the really hard way, it's up to you Paul."

He tried in vain to keep his mouth tightly shut so I walked over to my bench and lifted a large screw driver, I walked back over to Paul.

"Now are you sure you don't want to open up?" as I waved the screw driver in front of his face.

His eyes were wide open the fear in them, it was fantastic, he kept his teeth clenched together so I said, "Ok then let's get it open for you."

I forced the screw driver in through the side of Paul's face and with one good shove it came out through the other side. I wiggled the screw driver up and down until Paul screamed in pain and bingo.

"That's not too hard is it Paul?" With one hand prising his mouth open, I shoved one end of the hose down his throat, he was gagging and tears were now free flowing down his face. When I knew the hose was far enough down, I left him sitting there and walked back, as I stared at him, I lifted the bottle of bleach and shoved the end of the hose on it. I held it up and watched as the bleach started flowing down the tube, Paul could see it as well and he was helpless as he watched the bleach get closer and closer and then as it was now traveling down his throat, I knew he could feel it burning his insides. I must have let half the bottle go inside him before I stopped, I pulled the tube out of his throat and removed the screw driver as well, I stood back and waited to see the reaction and I wasn't prepared for what happened next.

Paul started heaving and then yep, up it came, only it was bright red with blood, he must have heaved for a good 5 minutes and he was covered in his own blood. He coughed and coughed and passed out, when he came back round, he was barely breathing, he was semi-conscious so I knew I hadn't got long left with him and stood there wondering how to finish him off.

I wanted to continue on my game with Porter and leave him another clue on who was next but I also wanted to keep a wee souvenir from Paul and my time with him, so as I stood there watching the life disappear from Paul, speak no evil came to mind, so I lifted my screw driver and put it in Paul's left ear I waited for him to open his eyes which was now a real struggle and as he did I said, "Say hello to Norman and Jason in Hell for me."

And I drove the screw driver into his brain, I watched as his pupils dilated and he was dead.

I went over to my bench and lifted Jonty's Bullet and a needle and thread, I placed the bullet in Paul's mouth and began to stitch his mouth shut, to be honest I made a mess of it but it was done and his mouth was tightly stitched shut.

I thought about what I would keep and decided I would have one of his hands, so I lifted the big butcher knife that I had and hacked off his left hand and set it on the bench alongside Jason's eye and one of Norman's ears, as I stood there looking at them I said, "Getting a nice wee collection going now but I will have to put yous in a jar to keep yous fresh." I would figure that out at some stage tomorrow but I now had to dump Paul's body and I knew the exact place I wanted to leave it, so I unstrapped his body and dragged him out to my van where I put him in, I went back inside and washed my hands that were covered in blood. I took a look at my clothes which also had blood stains on and knew then I would have to leave some clothes up here to get changed before I could leave the next time, I turned the light off and locked up, I got into my van and started the drive back down the Shankill.

After about a 10 minute drive, I had arrived, it was about 50 metres away from where I had lifted Paul off the road in the Shankill leisure centre car park. I positioned my van right in the middle of the car park and turned the engine off, I waited a minute or so to make sure the coast was clear and then I got out and opened the side door. I trailed Paul out and positioned him kneeling, I balanced his body so that his arms and body leant back and his body weight kept him up-right. I got into my van and drove away, it was perfect, he was on show to the whole world and I knew Porter would go nuts that another one of Sam's crew had been executed and left in such a public place, but most important was that Sam lost another one of his crew and that he would be now thinking who's next.

CHAPTER 11

The Pickled Eggs

I drove back up to my lock up and I was that buzzing, I decided to clean up. As I opened up, there was an eerie feeling about the whole place, it was so quiet, the rain had stopped and it was only me with my thoughts. I filled a bucket of water at the outside tap and poured it over the blood stained floor, I got the big yard brush and swept the floor but the blood had started to congeal and it was a bit sickening brushing the floor, but I knew I had to do it, I couldn't just leave it as there was too much evidence. The more I brushed, I just made the problem bigger, I decided to use the last of the bleach to try and clean the place up but it didn't make a difference. I did the best I could but I decided that the best plan was to burn the place to the ground after I finished killing. I locked up and got into my car and drove home, as I drove back down the road I could hear sirens and in the distance a blue flashing light, I parked just past

Agnes Street so I could see the whole way down to the leisure centre and when I saw a police car with its lights flashing and traveling at speed, I knew they had discovered the body. It took all my will power not to go down, but I knew with these blood stained clothes I would be caught, so it was a quick u-urn and back up home. I had just got in through the front door when the phone that Porter got me rang, I waited about 10 seconds before I answered it.

"Hello what's up?" I asked.

"Jonny its Porter, we have found another body and it's Paul, one of Sam's men, where are you?"

"I'm in bed, are you serious, it's Paul? Holy shit, did the I.R.A get him?"

"No Jonny, it's definitely not the I.R.A, we are dealing with something much worse," Porter sounded really worried.

"What do you mean worse?"

"This is a professional killing, it is connected with the other two so we are dealing with a serial killer and I fear you could be in danger, it looks like he is going through anyone connected with Sam."

"Calm down Porter, I'm not in any danger, are you going to release it that it isn't the I.R.A doing the killing? 'Cause if you don't Sam will go on the rampage."

"There will be a statement put out tomorrow but there are things about this killing that worries me."

He really had my attention now. "What do you mean, worries you?"

"I can't say Jonny but whoever is doing it is getting

good."

I smiled as I replied, "What do you need me to do?"

"Just stay safe and don't be walking anywhere at night, but most important again, I need any information if Sam is planning anything, can you do that Jonny?"

"Of course I can." I was really smug now and was really enjoying the game, I said goodbye and told Porter I would ring him later that day.

I stripped off and left my clothes in a pile beside the fire, I needed to burn them but was now that tired I would do it in the morning. I walked upstairs and washed my face and arms to get the blood off and got in to bed, I went out like a light, I was totally exhausted and slept right through till 1pm.

When I got up I went straight down stairs and lit the fire, I burnt each item of clothing and just sat there in my boxer shorts watching them burn, the different coloured flames fascinated me. As I sat there watching, I heard footsteps walk across my mum's bedroom floor, I jumped up and shouted, "Who's there?"

I got no answer, my heart was pounding, I caught out of the side of my eye a figure standing in the kitchen, I turned quickly and it was gone. I broke out in a sweat, my heart was thumping, I couldn't breathe, I gasped for air, my head was spinning. I fell back down onto the settee and tried to calm down, I just sat there watching the remains of my clothes burn, I told myself, "You're seeing things, your head is just playing tricks, calm down for Christ sake Jonny get yourself together."

I sat for a while and my stomach told me it's feeding time, when I went into the cupboard there was frig all in it and I remembered I didn't get to do the shopping because of the antics with Orange Lil so it was a drive down to Isabell's café for lunch and Sunday dinner. I sat alone in the corner and just listened to the other people in, it was all about Paul being murdered and someone even said that he was hacked to pieces and his body was all over the Shankill leisure centre car park, that humoured me as I tucked into roast beef with all the trimmings and extra gravy. The other customers were genuinely worried about who was next, I had missed the news on the TV but I overheard one of them saying that the Police are ruling out any involvement from the I.R.A and that they are looking for a single male in his late twenties of medium build and could possibly live in the vicinity of the Shankill road. I choked on a carrot and it went flying across the café, it actually hit a wee women on the back of the head and stuck in her hair, everyone looked round at me and one fella said, "Are you ok son?"

I nodded as I took a big drink of milk, nobody had noticed the carrot stuck in the wee woman's hair so I said nothing, I just finished off my lunch and paid my bill and left. It was now near 3pm and I knew I only had an hour left before I had to go into work but I needed to get some messages in and there was no way I was going into the *Co-op* so I drove over to East Belfast, I knew there was a few shops there I could get some shopping in.

I got what I needed and as I put them in the boot, I heard a familiar voice.

"Hi Jonny what has you over here?"

I turned immediately, it was Karen, she looked amazing I couldn't even speak I didn't even realise I was holding my breath.

"You look shocked to see me, are you ok Jonny?"

I exhaled. "Yeah, sorry Karen I was miles away there, I'm just getting a bit of shopping, how have you been?"

"Ok Jonny, just working away, why have you not rang me?"

I didn't know what to say and I don't know why I said what I did.

"I have been away for a while but I'm back now just getting myself together after my mum and nanny's funeral it's been hard but I'm coping better now."

"I'm glad you're doing ok, do you fancy going out for a drink sometime?"

My mind was racing, I wanted to meet Karen again but knew I couldn't, she would be in too much danger. As I looked her up and down, she was still as beautiful as I remembered her, I knew it was only about 4 months since I broke up with her but I still loved her, I just wish I could have told her everything but it had gone way too far now and I knew I had to finish it if I was ever to get closure.

"Karen I can't, not yet, I still need more time." My heart was ripping in two as I said that and looking at Karen, I knew she didn't understand.

She replied, "I won't wait forever Jonny, I have to get on with my life, you need to make your mind up you either want to be with me or not, or is there someone else?"

"No Karen there isn't, I swear," I replied.

If only I could tell her the truth, I thought.

"Then Jonny you need to be honest with yourself and honest with me, you know my number but then I suppose you won't ring."

And at that she just left me standing there holding a bag of shopping, I watched her walk off down the Newtownards Road and turn right into a street, I was gutted and annoyed with myself at the way I had treated her. I threw the bag of shopping into the boot and slammed it shut, I got into the car and drove back over to the Shankill and back home.

When I got into work, Billy and me got stuck into cleaning the bar. I lit the fire as it was bloody freezing and then began washing all the dirty glasses, the place was an absolute mess but we got through it and got it looking half decent again.

Billy and me talked about Paul's murder and it really concerned him about who could be next, he said, "Jonny this killer that is at large, it's really worrying me, it's like he is a ghost, nobody has seen or heard anything and he doesn't seem to want to stop."

"I know Billy, I hear they are looking for someone that could live on the road, they think he is in his twenties, they say he is a professional killer."

"I know Jonny, I wonder why he is targeting Sam's crew and if he is going to strike again, there is only Jonty and Sam left but I hear Sam has recruited more men in to protect him, but I'm sure they are bricking it."

"Aye Billy, I wouldn't want to be in their shoes, I wonder why he is killing members of the U.F.F he must be a psycho cause if they find out, he is a dead man."

"I think Jonny he must be on a death wish, he is a very brave man but as you say he must be a psycho."

"Do you want something out of the chippy Billy? I am starving."

"You took the words right out of my mouth, a couple of fish supers would be perfect, I will pay if you will go for them."

"Fair deal Billy," and at that Billy gave me a tenner and off I went to the chippers.

As I put my order in, I noticed on the counter a big jar with about 6 boiled eggs in it, I said to the girl, "How much are the eggs?"

She replied, "25p love, would you like one?"

"I will take them all but can I have the jar as well?"

I really didn't want the eggs, it was the jar I wanted, she replied, "Aye love but I would need 3 quid for it."

"Dead on," and at that I gave her the money.

On the way back up to work, I left the pickled eggs in the boot of my car and brought the fish and chips into the bar, Billy had a couple of pints set up and we sat and ate our dinner.

The pool team started arriving about 6.30 and it was the return leg of the local derby, the mountain view pool team were top of the league and if they won tonight, the league cup was theirs but if Heather Street won, it would go to a play off so tensions were high and as usual the drink was flying. It was really tight, it was 2 each with 7 games remaining so when Heather Street went 3-2 up, a big cheer went up as they were up to break and had the advantage. It went 4-2 then 5-2 and it looked like Heather Street was going to rump it but the Mountain View fought back and got it back to 5 each. With them to break up stepped their best player, his name was Davy, he was about 6 ft tall and heavy build, the only thing that struck me about him was his stench of B.O, he was stinking and the sweat patches on his white shirt were really noticeable. He hit the balls an almighty crack and 2 balls dropped in but he was in a bad position as he was tight up against the rail and stuck behind a yellow, so all he could do was play safe and at that up stepped a guy called Hammy. He was a good player as well and when he played he would bore the knickers of you, he was really slow, as he played the groans from the Mountain View crowd were very noticeable and it made the whole atmosphere terrible. I swear you could have cut it with a knife, the game must have took a good 20 minutes but when Hammy got down to the black and with Davy the Mountain View player having 5 reds left, it looked a formality. But then Hammy rattled the black and the crowd cheered, which caused a bloody row, drinks were spilt and punches were thrown. It took about 10 minutes to get everyone calmed down and Billy threw 4 of them out so when it was all calm again, Davy was able to play the game and he didn't miss a shot. He cleaned the heap and the Mountain View were crowned champions. They didn't stay long as it looked like there could have been a full flown digging match, so after all of that the Mount View team and supporters left and to be honest the rest of the ones there didn't really stay that long, they drank up and left. When I looked at my watch, it read 11.45 and happy days, an early night, Billy and me had a pint and as we were just about to lock up, Sam walked in with about 6 other men. He said to Billy, "Pour 6 pints and bring them into the back room,"

I just stood there glaring at Jonty and as he walked past me, he threw his shoulder into me and said, "Ball bag get the drinks in."

I absolutely hated him, he was a thug and he thought he was something now that he was Sam's second in command, he knew he could say or do anything. But oh, did I have plans for him, it was going to take a while because I had to get everything in place and pick my timing as it wouldn't be easy now that tensions were high and Sam and Jonty had minders everywhere they went so I got the drinks from Billy and brought them into the back room.

As I walked in I overheard Sam say, "So this killer that is at large, we have to find him and nut him, it's too close to home we need to put the word out and get him found."

My blood ran cold, if only they knew I was standing in front of them, Jonty looked at me funny and said, "Do you want a picture ball bag?"

I just glared at him for a split second, I could see his hair on fire and him screaming and his face covered in blood and then again he said, "Yo ball bag, are you fucking simple?"

I just blanked him and set the drinks down and turned and walked out, on the way out I could hear Jonty say, "I swear Sam that Jonny is fucking simple, there is definitely something not right there."

Sam replied, "Jonty forget about Jonny, we have to find this killer before he strikes again, that's our priority, now what I need to know is our safe house in Millisle still ok?"

I stopped in my tracks, I pretended to tie my lace as one of the men said, "Yes Sam I can get you the keys, why do you ask?"

Sam replied, "Jonty I want you off side, take a couple of weeks down there until this all gets sorted, we can't take any chances now."

Bingo, I thought, that's it, I will get him down there when his guard is down, I got up and walked over to Billy, "Is it ok if I shoot off Billy?"

"Aye Jonny, away you go, take tomorrow off I will see you at 5pm on Tuesday."

"Brilliant Billy see you then," and of I went, as I drove I got to the first corner and as I turned I heard the jar roll across the boot of my car. I braked and pulled over, the last thing I needed was my car stinking of pickled eggs, so I got out and lifted the jar out of the boot and set it in the front seat, I called into the kebab shop and got kebab on chips with extra sauce and a tin of *Coke* and headed home.

I sat there in my living room getting stuck into the kebab meat and it was lovely, it stunk of garlic but it was beaut, I washed it down with the tin of *Coke* and watched the TV and then the news came on and there stood Porter being interviewed. He was going on about a serial killer at large and if anyone had any information, to contact the police, he gave a brief description of a man they were looking for and my ears pricked up, I leant forward to listen.

He said, "We are looking for a man in his late twenties/early thirties with a medium build and was using a large vehicle, maybe a van to kidnap his victims and bring them to a derelict building, possibly a garage to kill them, if anyone sees anything suspicious don't approach the assailant as he would be armed and very dangerous, just contact the police."

I was that engrossed in what Porter was saying that I didn't even notice I spilt the bloody kebab sauce all over my jeans until it started burning. "Fuck," I said as I jumped up and I threw what was left of my kebab on the table and un buttoned my jeans to get them off. It bloody burned, I needed to get cold water on my legs so I shuffled across the floor to get to the sink, if I had of thought it out better I should have kicked my shoes off and removed my jeans but no not me. I walked across my living room floor at pace, I may say like a bloody penguin, and as I gained momentum into the kitchen I tripped, hit my head off the workbench and knocked myself out. I must have been out for about 2 hours, when I came round I was all groggy and felt sick, I got up and threw up in the sink which was still full of dishes, it was a bloody mess. I got myself together, kicked off my shoes and removed my kebab stained jeans and just went on up to bed. I fell into my bed and just went out cold.

I didn't wake until lunch time and when I did my head was thumping, I staggered into the bathroom, I swear you would think I was on the drink all night I felt that rough. As I looked at my reflection in the mirror and the bump I had on my forehead, I just stared and stared at what I saw in the mirror and to be honest, I didn't like what I saw, if my mum could only see what I had turned out to be she would be broken hearted.

I brushed my teeth and threw some water round my bake and got dressed, I went downstairs and started cleaning up, I heaved as I lifted and rinsed the dishes in the sink. I filled the kettle and made a cup of tea which helped wash down a couple of pain killers for my banging head, I spent a couple of hours cleaning the house and when I finished, it didn't look too bad, as I was in a cleaning mood I decided to go up Blackmountain and properly clean my kill room. I took a trip to the garage first to get some petrol in my car, as I went to pay the girl, I noticed petrol cans near the till. I bought a couple and filled them with petrol as well.

On the way back up the Shankill I took a chance and called into the *Co-op* to get more cleaning products, it was as quick as I could get round the shop. I would face 10 of big Sam but Orange Lil was a whole different ball game and I was relieved to get back into my car and be driving up the road.

When I arrived up at my kill room, something wasn't right, the hedges had been cut and as I pulled up a tractor was parked right outside the door. I stopped and got out, I walked round the back of the building and there stood Paddy, he walked over.

"Alright Brian how are you getting on, is business good?"

"Aye Paddy ticking over, what has you up here?"

"Up for some money Brian you still owe me for the other 4 months' rent."

"Oh right can you wait here and I will nip down home and get you your money, it's four hundred I owe you isn't that right?"

"Yes Brian it is and aye I can wait, I'm only up checking the place to make sure everything is ok."

"No worries Paddy, I won't be long."

And at that I got into my car, I have never drove down home and back again so quick, when I returned Paddy was sitting in his tractor just waiting on me, I gave him the 400 quid and he thanked me and said, "If you need the place longer it wouldn't be a problem, I could do another 6 months for 400 this time if you want."

I replied, "No worries Paddy I have a few weeks left so I will let you know," and at that Paddy drove off down the lane in his tractor.

I went straight over to the door and checked it hadn't been opened, a while back I had decided to tie a piece of thread round the lock every time I left so I would know if anyone had opened it but all good, Paddy hadn't been in. I always had my suspicions that he had an extra key and that worried me, I really should buy a different lock but I was nearly finished and with the petrol I bought I was going to burn the place to the ground after I was finished anyway.

I opened up and turned the light on, I went back

out to the car and brought in the jar with eggs in and set it on the bench. I opened it up and lifted out the eggs, I always wondered what they tasted like so I gave it a go and they were really strong tasting, it made me cough so I decided not to finish it. I lifted the other 5 out and binned them, I then lifted the ear, the hand and the eyeball I had kept and put them in the jar, the vinegar just about covered them and I put the lid back on. I stood back an admired the jar, I said, "You are an artist Jonny boy, a nice piece of work even if I do say so myself."

I went out to my car and brought in the cleaning products I had bought and started to clean the place up, it didn't take too long and it was as good as new. I put all my tools back in place and turned the light out and locked up, I tied the thread round the lock and I was ready for home.

CHAPTER 12

The Red Lion And A Wee Dance

When I got back down home, Billy was sitting outside in his car. I pulled up behind him and got out, he got out as well.

"Good timing Jonny, I was just about to give up on you."

"What's up Billy, is there something wrong?"

"No Jonny, what are you doing Friday till Monday?"

"Nothing Billy just work, why?"

"Well you won't believe it, I got you, me and a couple of my mates a trip to Benidorm, do you want to go?"

"Billy I would love to go but I haven't got a passport."

"That's not a problem, my mate in the passport office says he can get you one by Friday morning but we need to go now and it will cost you 50 quid."

"What about the bar Billy?"

"I have got cover in so we are good to go."

"Brilliant Billy, I could do with the break, hold on till I grab some money."

And at that I walked into the house, I went up the stairs 2 at a time and into my bag, I lifted out 300 quid and stuck it in my pocket and I went back out and in to Billy's car.

We stopped off to get my photo's done and then straight down to the passport office in town, Billy's mate was there and I filled in the form and gave him the 50 quid and 2 photo's he said to me, "I will give this to Billy on Friday morning, what time is your flight?"

I looked at Billy who replied, "We don't fly out till 3.40pm so we have loads of time."

"Spot on," the man said and Billy and me got back into his car.

As we drove back up the Shankill Billy said to me, "Jonny you are going to have to get some money changed, you need to go to the bank."

"How much should I take Billy?"

"A couple of hundred should do you 'cause we are all inclusive in the hotel."

"What's that Billy?"

"It means all your food and drink is paid for so you can fill your boots."

"Brilliant Billy I can't wait, I have never been

abroad before."

"Oh Jonny you are in for a treat when you get to the dorm, it's some spot."

"How much do I owe you Billy for the holiday?"

"Nothing Jonny, it's my treat you have been through the mill son and you deserve a bit of crack in your life/"

"Billy I couldn't do that, you need to take something for it."

"I tell you what you get the drinks in up at the airport and we will call it quits."

"No worries Billy, are you sure?"

"Yes Jonny I'm as much looking forward to it as you, Benidorm is the best place on the planet."

I got Billy to drop me off at the bank on the Shankill and I told him I would see him in work the following night.

I got 200 quid changed into euro's and it didn't look like real money but I got 300 euro for my money and on the way up the road I called in and bought myself a couple of pairs of shorts and a pair of swim shorts as well. As I walked back up home I had such a smile on my face, I was heading for Benidorm and I was on top of the world, I hadn't a care in the world and especially no interest in Jonty so I decided to bin Porter's phone. I wanted out, I didn't want to be part of killing anymore I loved this feeling and wanted more.

The next few days flew by and Friday morning I was up with the birds, I got a bit of breakfast and cleaned the house. Billy was to pick me up at 11 o'clock and he was bang on time, I lifted my bag and as I was locking the front door I said, "See you in a few days wee house." I smiled as I said that, it was like Christmas morning I was that excited, I got into Billy's car and he introduced me to his two mates.

"Jonny this is Hammy and Brian, my mates, they drink like fish so don't try and keep up you will end up paralytic." They all laughed and I knew I was in for a good weekend, I threw my bag in the boot and got into the car and we were off.

We had to meet Billy's mate in town to get my passport and when he gave me it I was chuffed to bits, my first passport and my ticket to anywhere, we were flying out of the international airport and it didn't take long to get there as the banter was flying in the car. Hammy was torturing me about some women called Vicky and a show she put on, he told me I would get my eyes opened.

We got booked in and got rid of our bags and headed for the bar, I got the first round in and we all got a fry as well, it was like a whole different world and I liked it. We had about 4 pints when our flight was called and we drank up and headed for the departure gate, it didn't take long and we were in our seats ready to take off. I was a bit nervous as I had never been on a plane before but when it accelerated, the adrenaline rush was fantastic, even better than killing and the threat of getting caught, we levelled off at about 30000 feet and then the drinks trolley came out. Billy was right, Hammy and Brian must have put away 10 vodka and cokes each and it didn't even fizz on them. I had a couple of beers just and we were nearly there, the captain told everyone to fasten their seat belts and as I looked out the window, the ground got closer and closer and thump and a big rev and we had landed in Spain.

It took about another 10 minutes or so but when they opened the doors, I walked down the steps and the heat hit me it was like when my ma opened up the oven door when she was cooking Sunday dinner. It was breath taking but I was so excited to be here, we collected our bags and headed for the bus.

I was star struck as I looked at the country side on the way up to Benidorm, it was a really beautiful country and then in the distance was the hotels of Benidorm, they were huge really tall buildings but beautiful with it. The closer we got, the more I could see the beach and the bars, it was just starting to get dark and all the bright lights of the bars were so noticeable and the girls, oh my God, they were all half naked. Billy was right this was the best place on the planet.

We arrived at our hotel, it was called the Sol Policanos and it was in the middle of Benidorm. Billy, Hammy and Brian must have been professionals at this as within 10 minutes of booking in, they were down in the bar and ready to go. I was just buzzing, we had one drink in the hotel and then headed for a bar called the Red Lion where this girl called Vicky was on.

We got a drink and sat near the front, the guy on the microphone started talking.

"And now for the main act of the night, please put your hands together for our one and only Sticky Vicky."

Everyone clapped and cheered, I looked at Billy, "Why do you call her Sticky Vicky?"

Hammy and Brian laughed their heads off Billy replied, "Wait and see Jonny," and he laughed as well.

The lights went down and then a single beam of light shone on the stage, I was fixated on the beam of light and then this awl doll came walking out with not a stitch on, the crowd whistled and cheered and I couldn't take my eyes off her and then she began to pull things out of her fanny. it ranged from flowers to lit light bulbs, she even got me to hold the end of a stream of bloody flags and I mean there must have been 10 flags I pulled out of her. I was traumatised but couldn't look away, it was brilliant, I was like a moth to a flame and then her finale was she opened up a bottle of coke and handed it to me to drink which got a huge cheer from Hammy, Brian and Billy, they loved it and to be honest it was as funny as it was filthy.

Hammy got a round of shots in which made me heave but I got it down anyway and we moved on to the next bar.

There was a comedian on called Tony Scott and he was hilarious, he came out singing a song and then just tortured everyone in the bar. He asked where everyone was from and when he shouted Northern Ireland we cheered, he then said to everyone and pointed to us, "When they leave, we all leave." The bar burst out laughing at our expense, I may add but it was good crack, some big girl at the front got ripped apart, he absolutely gave her a mauling but she took it in good fun and the night was now in full throttle. Bar after bar, drink after drink and I think we called it a night about 4 in the morning, I was absolutely wrecked but made it home and into bed.

I woke up the next morning feeling rough, my head was thumping and I could of threw up but there was only one thing to do, jump in the pool and fight back.

I got my shorts on and lifted a hotel towel and said to Billy I would see him at breakfast. I got into the lift and it made me feel ill as it went down, I staggered through reception, I think I was still half cut but when I walked out into the pool area it was bunged and I felt a thousand eyes on me. I checked myself to make sure nothing was hanging out and walked over to the pool, I set my towel on a wall and jumped into the pool, it took my breath away, it was bloody freezing and when I came up I actually gave a scream out which got a laugh from everyone round it, that's why they were looking at me and I bet you they were hoping I would jump in. I got out as quick as I got in and grabbed my towel and got dried, one girl lying on a sun bed and I may add, she was topless sat up and said, "A bit cold the pool?"

I was shivering, I replied, "COLD? it's bloody Baltic?" I couldn't take my eyes off her, she was quite pretty I asked her, "What's your name?"

She replied, "Susan, I'm from Manchester, what's your name?"

"I'm Jonny and I'm from Belfast."

"Oh right, I take it this is your first time in Benidorm?"

"Why do you ask?"

"You can just tell, your shorts are back to front and everyone knows you can't get into the pool until after lunch until it heats up."

I looked down and yep, bloody shorts back to front, I was scundered I replied, "Aye I haven't been abroad before but it's some spot."

She asked, "Have you been to the black chicken yet?"

"No we only arrived last night, what's the black chicken?" I asked.

"It's a karaoke bar, get your mates to take you, you will love it, me and my mates are going later about 4 if you fancy it?"

"Yeah no worries, I will see you there."

At that I went back up to my room to get changed and go for breakfast, Billy was already dressed so I threw a dry pair of shorts on and a tee shirt. I stuck my trainers on and we left and went to meet Hammy and Brian.

We all got a big fry up each and it was a real struggle just getting it down, but I felt better after it and we were out on the lash again.

The first bar we went to was a Rangers bar, all the loyalist tunes were playing, we might as well have been on the Shankill road but the crack was good. I could just manage a pint but Hammy, Brian and Billy had 2 pints and a couple of vodkas each, they really were hard-core. Billy said to me, "Jonny your cure is in the bottom of your second glass."

Hammy and Brian laughed and Hammy said, "Aye Jonny get them down you, I will get you a wee cure," and at that Hammy went up to the bar.

I said to Billy, "I'm struggling Billy, I feel like crap."

"You will be fine Jonny, another couple of drinks and a bit of lunch and you will be back on form."

At that Hammy came down from the bar with 4 shots, he set one each in front of us and said, "Right lads, down in one."

We all lifted our glasses and down the hatch they went, I started coughing, it was really strong I said as I caught my breath, "What the fuck was that Hammy?"

He laughed as he replied, "It's just a wee rumple mint it's like one of your five a day." We all laughed and it actually worked, I felt a lot better and as penny arcade came on, we all started singing.

We stayed about another hour and then went to the chippers for lunch, we were all steaming again and I'm sure if anybody looking at us they would have said, look at the state of them, but we didn't care we were on a roll again.

It was now about 3.30 so we decided to head round to the black chicken and Susan was right, it was buzzing and again the drink was flying. Hammy got up and sang on the karaoke, it was a Neil Diamond track, *Sweet Caroline,* and the crowd loved it. The place was bouncing, just as Hammy was finishing his song Susan and her mates walked in, she waved over and I waved back. Billy said to me, "Aye aye Jonny, you're a dark horse, how do you know her?"

My face went red and I replied, "Met her this

morning round the pool."

"She's a looker Jonny, you're in there son."

"Don't think so Billy," at that Susan and her mates came walking over.

"Can we join you boys, there doesn't seem to be any other tables free?"

"Course yous can," I replied as Billy gave me an elbow to the ribs.

Brian said, "What are your names?"

"This is Anne, Margret and I'm Susan," she replied.

My face was a pure red'ner but we all shifted round and the girls sat down, Susan sat beside me just as Hammy came down.

"Oh aye, I'm just away for a couple of minutes and I'm blew out already."

Everyone laughed and moved round a bit more to let Hammy in.

A few more drinks later and a couple of bad singers and the crack was brilliant, Susan was really nice but she wasn't Karen and I sat for a while over a pint thinking how much I missed her, then Susan said to me, "You're miles away Jonny, is there something wrong?"

I looked round and smiled.

"No Susan, just a bit drunk," at that I heard my name being called for a song, I shrunk down in my seat hoping nobody else heard but not my luck, they all cheered as it was called again and pushed me up as I staggered over to the guy that was running the Karaoke.

He asked me, "What would you like to sing son?"

My mind went blank, I hadn't a clue and then yep, out it came, "*The Gambler* by Kenny Rodgers."

As the song started, my face was on fire but when I got going I actually enjoyed it and the crowd gave a big cheer when I finished. I went and sat down and Susan leant over and gave me a kiss on the cheek and said, "You were very good at that Jonny."

Billy and the boys gave a cheer and Hammy whistled as Susan kissed me again and I was pure scundered she said to me, "Don't be worrying about them they are just jealous, will you meet me later?"

"Aye," I replied. "Where will yous be?"

"We are heading to the Red Lion, there is a hypnotist on tonight at eleven and I hear he is very good."

"Yeah we will be there."

Susan and her friends said goodbye and left, Billy turned round to me and said, "You're in there Jonny, fill your boots son."

Hammy and Brian laughed and Hammy said to Billy, "I hate to see the one you're getting Billy, you are taking one for the team." Brian was laughing his head off.

"No chance Hammy, I'm too old for that crap, you work away mate."

"Jonny it's your round get them in," Hammy said.

"Hammy we will head up the town and have one more in uncle Ped's before we go for dinner, Jonny here won't last the night if we stay here any longer,"

Billy said.

"Aye alright we don't want lover boy not able to perform." That got a laugh from everyone and we drunk up and headed up to Ped's.

As we walked up, I was staggering all over the place but I made it to the next bar, I just had a *Coke* because I was really drunk and Billy told me to take it easy.

We got back up to the hotel and I fell into bed and went unconscious, I must have slept for 2 hours, it was the sound of Billy singing in the shower that woke me. I looked at my watch and it was now 9.30.

"Holy shit," I said.

At that Billy came out of the bathroom, with not a stitch on.

"Fuck sake Billy put some clothes on," I said.

"Wise up Jonny we all have one, now go in and get a shower and freshen yourself up, you have a big date tonight."

"No chance Billy, I'm not interested just here for the beer."

Billy laughed, "You're a poet and you don't know it Jonny."

I went in and had a shave and a shower and got dressed, slapped a bit of aftershave on and I was good to go.

We met Hammy and Brian down in the dining room where we had a quare feed and we were ready for the town.

When we walked up main street, it was bunged

every bar was bouncing there was even some head cases dressed up, we even saw Batman and Robin, it was hilarious 'cause Batman was a dwarf and Robin was about 6ft tall, it made my night. Then we called into a bar where we done a couple of rounds of shots and we were off again, the banter was flying and it was Brian's turn we all jumped on, Hammy was torturing him about his dodgy moustache, he told him he looked like a porn star, he didn't take it too good so I think that's why he got a ripping.

It was now close to 11 so we headed round to the Red Lion, when we got in there was standing room only so we got a space at the bar and got the drinks in. The hypnotist came on and he started by getting everyone to join their hands together and put them fingers down on top of their own heads, we all done it for a laugh but when he counted backwards from 10 and then told everyone to release their hands mine was bloody stuck, for the life of me I couldn't pull them apart, Billy and the lads stood there laughing but I was really panicking, I was asked along with 9 other people to go up on stage where we all sat on seats and the hypnotist released our hands.

He explained what had happened and then one by one he put us all to sleep, I was the last one he did and I was sure it was a bluff but nope, he touched me on the forehead and I was out like a light.

When I came round some boy beside me was eating an onion and holy God he was really enjoying it, the smell of it was hectic but he asked him if he was enjoying the nice apple and chump chump, the guy ate the heap, the crowd was in stitches, he then came over to me and touched my forehead and that's the last thing I remembered.

When I came round I was thanked and told to go back and join my mates, I walked over thinking that wasn't too bad but the look on the lads faces told me something wasn't right as I got up to them I said, "Well what happened?"

Billy replied, "Nothing Jonny he couldn't hypnotise you." Hammy and Brian stood there laughing, I knew something wasn't right, just then some music came on it was classical and for some strange reason I grabbed some girl and started slow dancing her round the floor, I couldn't stop. I burled her a couple of times and then the music stopped, I was standing in the middle of the floor not knowing what to think, the crowd was laughing, I could feel my face burning. I walked back over to Billy and the lads and lifted my pint, they didn't even speak they were in ruptures, the magician asked if I was ok and I just nodded he then said, "Jonny have you lost something?" and fuck I felt down and my dick was missing, I ran round the whole bar asking who had it but nobody did, I was furious some fucker here had stolen it and if I found out I would do them in. I think the magician knew I was getting really annoyed so he came up to me and clicked his fingers and I was out. I woke up on the floor on top of some girl and some fella on top of me, the crowd was laughing their heads off, I wasn't too well pleased and threw the guy off me. I got up and walked back over to Billy but the bloody classical music came on and I was off again, I could do nothing but bloody twirl some girl round the floor, I kept looking over at my mates who had tears now running down their face. When the music stopped, I realised it was Susan I was dancing with and we both just stood there and laughed, she gave me a hug and a kiss which got a cheer from the crowd and I swear I heard Hammy give a big wolf whistle. I was scundered but had a laugh with it.

I walked back over to the lads and glanced at my watch, bloody 12.30 I said to Billy, "Have you seen the time?"

"Aye Jonny you were hilarious there, brilliant mate just brilliant."

"I can't remember any of it mate, what happened?"

"You don't need to know Jonny," Hammy said and we all stood there laughing.

A couple more drinks and we went to leave, as we walked out Susan and her mates were outside she called me over.

"Jonny that was really funny would you like to come back to my hotel for drinks?" and she winked.

I had seen that wink before, bloody Orange Lil and the memories hunted me, I replied, "Susan I have to say no I hope you understand, there is a girl back home."

"Fair play to you, Jonny you could have said nothing and just came back, she is a lucky girl," and at that she leant in and gave me a kiss on the cheek.

I walked back over to the lads and Hammy said, "What's wrong Jonny, have you still lost your dick?" and they all laughed.

"Aye something like that," I replied.

Billy said, "Where are we going now Hammy?"

"Round to the rock club, there is a quare singer on the night."

So off we went and Hammy was right, it was a good night and I surprised myself I kept up with them rightly it was again about 4am when we got to bed.

The next day I thought just a wee quiet one but no we headed to the bar on the beach called Tiki Beach and when we got there it was in full throttle, two guys were on singing and I thought they could drink back on the Shankill but here was a whole different league, the bottles of beer were flying cocktails, shots, oh my God everyone was blocked again and it was a full on party it was brilliant. We ordered 2 buckets of beer and with it being my round, I was gob smacked that it only cost 10 euro, 14 bottles of beer and only 10 euro, any wonder everyone was blocked. We sat there and the lads were still slagging me about last night and then this guy came over and introduced himself as a street entertainer, we all looked at each other and then he began to show us card tricks, he was very good but it was when he asked for my watch it totally shocked the shit out of me, he placed it in his hand and told me to watch the second hand tick so I did and then he said, "Just tell it to stop," so I did and holy God the bloody watched stopped.

He handed it back to me and went to walk off, I shouted after him, "Hey boy, my watch isn't working."

He replied, "Just tell it to start."

So I did and that was the bit that shocked me, it just started working again, I sat down and all of us were amazed, he was brilliant. We sat and drank our beer and sang along with the two guys that were singing and had a quare laugh, I sat there and just looked round me, I said to Billy, "Does nobody work Billy, Benidorm is bunged?"

He just laughed, "Aye Jonny, I told you it's some spot."

We ordered hamburgers and chips and of course more drink, there was a stag party in and what made it worse, there was a hen party in as well. The guys were all dressed as women which was hilarious, one of them had a thong on and I swear his balls were hanging out either side of his knickers, he was bunkers but loved the attention from the girls who I may add weren't wearing much either, but then again anything goes in Benidorm.

We sat on drinking and then more street entertainers came in, they were acrobats and they put on a show, their finale was four of them all standing one on top of the other on their shoulders, they were fit boys. I said to Hammy, "Here Hammy they would be quare window cleaners, they wouldn't need a ladder."

We all laughed and were in full flow now, we started on the vodkas so by 6pm we were blocked again and had to head back to the hotel for some dinner and try and sober up a bit.

Sunday night was as bad as the previous two, we just went from bar to bar and watched a few of the shows, we bumped back into the stag and hen party who were now all drinking together. They were all wrote off and it was really funny to watch as the guys were touching for the girls and with them all in dresses and the guy's makeup a mess, it was good crack to see, we had another good night and to be honest by Monday I was burnt out and was ready for home.

Lunch time Monday and Billy said to me, "Jonny we are bringing back some cigarettes is that ok with you?"

"Aye Billy how many do you need me to take?"

"Thirty cartons, get as many into your case and then I have bought you a carry-on bag so we will fill that as well."

"Yeah that's dead on Billy."

So we went round to the tobacconist and Billy bought 120 cartons of silk cut, we split them between us and filled the bags, we got picked up about 5pm and we were off home.

Our flight was 9pm and we arrived back in Belfast for 11pm, as we collected our bags we had to walk through customs and this big peeler looked at me funny but didn't stop me. We all got into Billy's car and Billy dropped me off, I emptied my cigarettes into Billy's boot and thanked them all for a super weekend.

I got in through my front door and just fell into the settee, it was so comfortable. I sat and recalled the previous 3 days and had a laugh, it really was a great few days but I was burnt out and headed for bed.

CHAPTER 13

24 Hours

The next morning, I was woken by loud knocking at my front door, I jumped out of bed and went straight downstairs to open it.

As I walked down the stairs, the knocking got louder and I shouted, "Hold your horses I will be there in a minute."

The knocking stopped, as I opened the door a peeler grabbed me and put me on the settee I shouted at him, "Get your fucking hands off me."

He replied, "Shut your mouth and just sit there."

As I looked round another two peelers came in and along with them was Porter, when I saw him I said, "What the fuck Porter, what's going on?"

He replied, "Jonny you have been a bad boy and I'm not happy about it."

My heart was thumping, a big lump in my throat

and my mouth was so dry, my mind was racing, did he know that it is me doing the killing? I spoke up, "What do you mean?"

"Where's the phone I gave you? And why did you fuck off to Benidorm without telling me?"

Panic over, he didn't know I replied, "I lost the phone I think someone stole it in the bar and you're not my da, I think you will find I can go where I like."

He didn't take that too well, he turned to the peeler and said, "Take him in I'm fed up with his shit."

"Woah, wait Porter, I didn't mean that I'm just tired."

"Too late Jonny, just take him," Porter said to the peeler again.

At that, the big peeler grabbed me and put me on the floor, he grabbed my hands and put them behind my back and put handcuffs on, the fucker put them that tight they were hurting me. I shouted out to Porter again, "What the fuck Porter? It doesn't have to be like this get these fucking cuffs off me."

The peeler grabbed me by the hair and lifted me off the ground, he marched me outside and put me in the back of a car and the fucker hit my head off the side of the car as he did it, I cried out, "Fuck sake there is no need Porter, we are finished."

Porter opened the door again and said, "Indeed we are Jonny, you are going away for a while." He then slammed the door and tapped the roof, the peeler in the front then drove off, I looked round as we drove down my street, a few of the neighbours were out and as I stared at Porter standing at my front door, I wondered if I would see my wee house again and it worried me if Porter found my money and guns.

We drove up the motorway and as I sat in the back of that car, I wondered where they were taking me, I said to the peeler in the front, "Where you taking me?"

He didn't even answer, he didn't even take me under his notice.

"There is no need to be ignorant."

Again he never flinched, I looked at the signs as we were driving up past Mullusk and then about another 15 minutes, he took a turn off to Antrim. We drove for about another 5 minutes and then turned left into a building that had a large wall round it and a security gate at the front of it. A soldier who was carrying a machine gun opened the gate, we drove on in and parked in front of the building, the peeler got out and opened up my door, as I sat there only in my boxer shorts I could feel the cold air hit my body and I started shivering. The handcuffs were cutting the wrists off me and then the peeler grabbed me again by the hair and trailed me out of the car, I fell out of it hitting the cold wet concrete ground and cutting my face in the process. "Fuck me I can fucking walk you know?"

Again the peeler lifted me off the cold ground by the hair and trailed me into the building where he put me in a dark room with a single chair in it, he slammed the door behind him leaving me there in total darkness.

I don't know how long I was sitting there just in my own thoughts and I kept going back to the times I had spent with Karen, they were happy times and I just sat with my eyes closed. I just wished all the bad times to go away but they now haunted me, flashes of Norman, Jason and Paul kept rushing round my head, I shook my head a few times but visions of their dead bodies were as clear as day and it was only when the door opened and the lone figure of Porter stood there that the visions stopped. I looked at him and said, "Porter what is going on I thought we had a deal?"

"Oh we did Jonny, but you broke that deal the minute you trashed the phone."

"I told you I think someone stole it, I swear Porter I couldn't contact you as I didn't write your number down."

"Well Jonny things have moved on from there and I think you need to start talking."

"What do you mean Porter?" I was getting really nervous the way he was talking, it was like he knew it was me.

"How's your van driving? Is the battery still charged?"

Fuck he knew, he knew everything. "What are you talking about?"

"Your van Jonny, your wee white van that is parked up Blackmountain right as we speak?"

"Tell me what you know Porter?"

"Oh Jonny I know it all," at that Porter turned and walked out, he slammed the door and again I was left alone in the dark.

I could hear my heart thumping, I was gasping for air, I was caught and I didn't know what to do, was this it?

As I sat there, a tear ran down my cheek and my face smarted as it rolled over the cut on my face. I was finished, I just lowered my head and just sat waiting for Porter to return.

I must have fell asleep as when I woke it was so quiet, I was still sitting in the same spot and my neck was bloody aching. I rolled my head round to try and relieve the pain, the door opened and Porter walked in holding a file.

"Right Jonny, this is how it is, there is only my team know you are here so your secret is safe with us, we want you to finish the job."

"What do you mean Porter?" I said in shock.

"I mean we want you to finish the job, we want these bastards taken out and we know you have plans to do it."

"If I do it I will need to get away somewhere far and I would need money to start a new life."

"I understand that Jonny, we will get that sorted after you are finished but we need assurances that it's clean and both Jonty and Sam are executed, forget about leaving their bodies in a public place, we just want them dead, do you understand that?"

I didn't know what to think, he knew I was the killer and he wasn't going to arrest me and the most important thing was that he wanted me to continue.

"What happens now then?" I asked.

"You go back to your normal life and finish what you have started, we want this ended."

"What if I don't want to do it?"

"Then you're fucked son, you will be going away for a very long time, we have enough evidence to bury you, so I don't see you have a choice." At that he threw the file on my lap, I looked down and it read Jonny Andrews.

He was right I was fucked, no matter what I did, but then I was going to get the chance to kill Jonty and Sam.

"Ok I will do it but I have conditions of my own."

Porter looked at me as I told him how it was going to end and he agreed to everything I wanted.

As he unlocked the handcuffs and gave me a boiler suit to put on, we walked outside which was pitch black, a car was waiting for me which I got into and it drove me home.

I was just getting into my house as the sun was coming up and I went in and put the kettle on and had a couple of rounds of toast, I sat watching the blank screen of the TV eating my breakfast, making plans for Jonty.

.

CHAPTER 14

The Trip To Millisle

I went upstairs and got a shower and even though the water was cold it felt good, I could only stick it for a bit and got out and got dried. I put on my good jeans and a nice shirt, I had decided in the time I had spent in that darkened room that I wanted to see Karen again as I didn't know, once this started, if I would ever see her again and I needed to know if I did come out of this alive, would I ever have her by my side again.

I rang her house and her mum answered.

"Hello Sandra, it's Jonny, could I speak with Karen if she is in?"

"Aw, hello Jonny, you are in luck, today is her day off, I think she is still in bed hold on and I will give her a shout."

At that I heard Karen's mum shout on her and I heard Karen answer back, she then lifted the phone.

"Hi Jonny how are you?"

"Yeah I'm ok, how have you been?"

I then heard Karen shout to her mum to put the other phone down, she then said to me, "See my ma, she always listens in to my conversations, she does my head in."

I just laughed and then asked her, "Karen would you like to go for a drive today?"

"I would love to Jonny, it's been too long not seeing you."

"I know Karen I have missed you as well, I will pick you up in about an hour if that's ok?"

"Yeah that's fine, do I need to bring anything?"

"No Karen, just yourself."

"See you shortly Jonny," Karen replied and she hung the phone up.

I tided the house a bit just to put the time in and then I left to go and pick Karen up, on the drive over I had the music pumping and the window down a bit, the cool air was circulating round the car and as I drove down Karen's street someone must have just cut their grass cause the smell was lovely, a real fresh scent, if only you could bottle that smell I would have it as an air freshener I thought.

I pulled up outside Karen's house and tooted the horn, a couple of minutes passed and out Karen came, she had the most beautiful smile I didn't even know what she was wearing as I was so fixated on her smile. She opened the passenger door and got in she leant across and we kissed, it wasn't a full on snog just a peck and then she said, "Well where are we going

Jonny?"

"I thought what about a wee drive down to Millisle, I hear it's nice down there?"

"Yeah Jonny that sounds nice."

As we drove off, Prince came on the radio and Karen said, "Turn that up Jonny, I love Prince."

I replied, "Are you joking? He's a freak."

"No way Jonny, he's brilliant, you have to listen to him his music is something else, if he ever came to Belfast or Dublin I would go."

"You're not right in the head, he is weird looking, what size is he about 5ft? And with all that makeup he is definitely not of this world, I swear if there are aliens on this planet he is one of them."

Karen laughed, we just fell into the old routine and it was great, I didn't realise that I had missed her so much.

We drove down through Newtownards and I recalled the time we played a match down there and it brought back some nice memories. We took the coast road, it was beautiful, the scenery was stunning, we drove along the road, Strangford Lough was on our right and looking across you could see the Mourne Mountains, they were stunning. I said to Karen, "Remember our day down in Newcastle?"

"Yes Jonny I do," she answered as she looked at her left hand, I noticed she wasn't wearing her engagement ring but then I couldn't expect her to wait on me forever. It was just nice us two driving and chatting, she put her hand down and turned and looked out the side window, it felt awkward but as we drove into a place called Greyabbey and turned left towards Millisle, I said, "Karen you know my life has been a struggle but when I'm with you nothing matters, I know now that I need you in it, to be honest I could leave the Shankill and run away somewhere far."

As I said that Karen turned to me and said, "Jonny that's all well and good but you have treated me like crap and to be honest we need to take things slow for a while."

"I know Karen, I know I have but I wasn't thinking straight, but being with you again I know now how I feel about you and never want to let you go again."

"We will give it time and we will see where it goes," Karen replied.

As we arrived in Millisle, I parked at the beach, we got out of the car and walked onto the soft golden sand. We held hands and wandered along the beach, we chatted about work and just each other's life, Karen still went out on Thursday nights with a few friends to the Botanic Inn up in Belfast, which was good that she still kept in contact with them. She asked me if I ever went out and I told her that I was just back from Benidorm with Billy and a couple of his mates, I told her about the bars there and about being hypnotised we laughed about it and Karen said she would have loved to go and that it sounded good fun.

We walked up the town and called in to get an ice cream, Karen got a mint choc chip one but mine, oh my God, it was gorgeous it was strawberry and double cream. I had never tasted anything like it before in my life, I swear I was talking to it when I ate it, we sat on the wall just at the beach and looked across the ocean, in the distance you could see land. I said to Karen, "I wonder where that is?"

She replied, "I think it's Scotland."

"No way," I replied. "Is it that close?"

"Yeah it's only a couple of hours on the boat."

I thought to myself frigging hell that's not far enough away, if I have to move to there after this is finished, I probably would be on a U.F.F hit list so I would need to speak with Porter about where I was going to escape too.

We finished our ice-cream and took a dander back down the town, we called into an arcade that was open and played a couple of fruit machines, as we stood there playing the machines, Karen said to me, "Jonny, today has been nice I have really enjoyed being out with you again."

"Yeah I know Karen, I feel the same."

Just at that Karen filled 3 bells and won the Jackpot five quid, and the look on her face was priceless, she was screaming with joy, the guy that run the place came over.

"Jesus love, I thought there was something wrong," he laughed as he realised Karen had won the jackpot. "Well done love, that's a nice wee win for you."

I looked round, "Thanks mate it's made our day."

Karen was chuffed to bits she said to me, "That's lunch sorted Jonny, we will go to the chippy."

I smiled, "What, lunch and your buying? I'm up for that."

We left and walked a couple of doors down and into the chippers, we got a table by the window and the girl came over and took our order. Karen ordered two battered sausages and chips and I got my usual, a fish supper, we both got tea and a couple of rounds of bread and butter. We sat chatting and it wasn't long before our lunch came, I plastered mine in salt and vinegar, Karen said to me, "Would you like some chips with that salt and vinegar Jonny?"

I laughed, "I know Karen, I love the taste of chippy vinegar." I looked at my plate and I think the chips were swimming across it, I think I over done it a bit but a slice of bread and a few chips and I mopped it up, as I took a bite, the vinegar caught my throat I coughed, Karen laughed.

"I knew you put too much on, you header."

I laughed as well, we sat there eating and as I glanced out the window, I saw a familiar face, Jonty.

He was walking by holding a couple of bags of shopping, as he looked into the chippy I quickly looked away, I didn't want him to see me. I glanced back and he was away, Karen looked at me and said, "What's wrong Jonny, you look like you have seen a ghost?"

"Nothing Karen, I'm fine," and I filled my fork with a big whack of fish and put it in my mouth, it was gorgeous I horsed the rest of it into me and sat and drank my tea waiting for Karen to finish.

When we finished our lunch I really wanted to see where Jonty had gone to, but when we walked up the town, there was no sign of him. I said to Karen, "Do you want to head on, I have to work tonight?"

"Yeah Jonny, no worries, I have had a lovely day."

We walked back to the car park and got into my car, as we drove up the town I spotted Jonty coming out of a bar, I slowed down and let a woman cross the road. Karen said to me, "You're a nice fella Jonny, that wee women would never get across the road." Little did she know I was just interested to see were Jonty was going.

I replied, "Thanks Karen, she looks like she was struggling there." As I watched Jonty turn down a side street, I was able to drive on, I went slowly as I watched him go into the second door on the left down the street and I smiled, got him, I thought.

We drove on down through Donaghadee and headed for Bangor, as we left Donaghadee, Karen commented, "Jonny aren't them houses beautiful?"

I replied, "Oh my God, they are mansions you would have to be a millionaire to have one of them."

As we drove up the road, my mind was on overtime, I now knew he was down here and knew exactly the house he was in and hopefully alone.

We drove into Bangor and out through the ring road and headed for Belfast, we chatted on the way up the carriageway, Karen said to me, "Jonny would you like to go out next week sometime?"

"Yeah Karen I would like that, when do you want to meet?"

"Me and a few friends are heading out to the Bot on Thursday night if you fancy it?"

"Yeah defo count me in, what time?"

"We usually head in for about 9 or so."

"That's great sure, I will meet you there."

As I left the carriageway and drove down the Hollywood Road, I was smiling, a song came on the radio and the two of us just sang along, it was just like old times. I dropped Karen off home but not before I stole a snog, she smiled and said, "See you next Thursday then Jonny."

"You can count on it," I replied as she closed the door and I drove off.

As I drove over to the Shankill I now was thinking about Jonty and I knew I wouldn't have long before he would be back to the Shankill and back to the safety of the U.F.F so it had to be done this weekend and to be honest, I wanted all this finished before I met Karen on Thursday night.

CHAPTER 15

The Strippers

That night in work we had a birthday party in and you would think a Wednesday night would be a bad night for a party, but no, not on the Shankill, that's one thing that the people on the Shankill could do and that's throw a good party.

It was a fortieth birthday and the girl was called Paula, she was quite small and to be honest a bit heavy but she looked well in her tight fitting dress, she had got her hair done up in a bun and I thought to myself, who ever done your makeup love done a good job, as it made her look quite pretty. The room was done up with banners and balloons, there was champagne for everyone when they arrived but to be honest I don't know where Billy got it from, I tasted it and it was bloody stinking the only thing I would use that for was to clean the toilets but they all seemed to enjoy it. By 9 o'clock it was in full swing, the DJ was brilliant, he played all the right music having the floor bunged, there must have been close to a hundred people in and we were slaughtered behind the bar, it was like a Saturday night we were that busy. I turned to Billy and said, "Frigging hell Billy, this is nuts."

"I know Jonny I wasn't expecting it to be this busy, we are going to run out of bottled beer soon so try and talk them into pints."

I looked at Billy and said, "Billy the women won't drink pints."

"Of course they will Jonny if there are no bottles left they will drink anything."

Billy was right, once the bottles ran out they didn't even complain, the pints were then flowing which was good as it took them longer to drink.

I looked up at the clock and it read 11pm and at that, two fellas came up to the bar, one of them was very heavy and small with not much hair either, the other one was about 6ft well-built and very tanned, he looked like he was just of the plane from Spain. The fat one asked Billy, "Is there somewhere we can get changed."

"Why do you ask?" Billy replied.

"The birthday girl's mate has ordered a stripper so we need to get ready."

"Oh right you will have to use the back room," Billy pointed over to the door and the two guys both carrying bags walked over and went into the back room.

After about ten minutes, the muscly guy came over and said to Billy, "Can you put this tape on? When I gave you the nod, press play."

"Yeah no worries mate, I will get the DJ to do it for you, he will give you a mike as well."

"That would be perfect."

Billy turned to me and handed me the tape, "Jonny go and tell the DJ to play it when he is ready."

"No worries Billy." At that I walked over to the DJ and explained what was going to happen.

The D.J handed the guy the mike and when the song that he was playing finished, he gave the guy the nod.

The muscly guy went and put a single chair in the middle of the dance floor and then lifted the mike, he then said, "I believe there is a young lady here tonight celebrating a special birthday," The crowd cheered and Paula's mates ushered her to the chair, Paula put up a bit of a struggle but was sat down in the middle of the room, the house lights came on and god love her she was absolutely scundered her face was beaming.

The muscly guy walked over and started talking, "Well Paula, you are in for treat tonight," he leant down and gave her a kiss on the cheek which got a huge cheer from the crowd, he then turned to the DJ and nodded. At that the DJ put the music on and it was one by Joe Cocker, I think you called it *You Can Leave Your Hat On*, he then set the mike down and started dancing in front of her. He took his shirt off, the women in the crowd all cheered, he was some shape his muscles even had muscles, he rubbed himself up against Paula who was now starting to enjoy it. Her hands were rubbing his chest and then he ripped his trousers off, the place went wild, the whistles and cheers from the crowd was deafening. Paula was really up for it now her hands were all over him and then he stopped dancing, he said, "Now Paula, calm down." He then walked over to the D.J and lifted a length of black fabric and danced back over again, putting the fabric in-between his legs and moving it really sexually, Paula couldn't contain herself, she was rubbing her hands together and the smile on her face was huge. There was no more shy Paula, this girl was up for anything, he danced over and then started putting the fabric round Paula's neck and pulling her head down towards his just about covered dick, she was loving it. He then let her up again, as the song just finished he tied the fabric round Paula's eyes and she didn't even struggle, he then said to her that he wanted her to put body lotion anywhere she wanted to put it on him but she wasn't allowed to look just touch only.

Another song came on, he then nodded over to the door at the back room, the other stripper came dancing over, the crowd cheered as he got to the dance floor Billy and me were in ruptures he didn't look like a stripper when he had his clothes on and now that he had only the same thong on that the big muscly guy had on. He was horrific looking, he had a big fat belly, a hairy back, he was about 5ft tall with a nearly bald head but wow could he move, he was a real wee dynamo. The crowd were in full tilt they were cheering, laughing and whistling which just made him dance even more, as he got over to Paula, the muscly gut handed him a bottle of body lotion and he really sexually poured it over his chest and fat belly, he took Paula's hands and placed them on his chest and god love Paula, she didn't have a clue. She was rubbing his chest feeling every inch of his body, and I mean every inch, she rubbed the body lotion everywhere he even turned round and she rubbed it into his bum, the crowd was going wild and Paula was getting a bit too excited and I think when she felt his hairy back, the penny dropped. She took off the blind fold and let a scream out of her and then she was in kinks of laughter she took it in good fun, the two strippers then started dancing round her and the fat one straddled her and rubbed her face in his chest and when she lifted her head back, the bloody body lotion was all over her face and her hair was now every shape they really did give her a going over. The song finished and the crowd cheered, both the strippers gave her a kiss and when the fat one gave her a kiss, he bent her backwards and I swear we never laughed as much in our lives as he bent her backwards, the two of them fell on the floor with the fat man on top of Paula. It was a total train wreck, someone shouted from the crowd, "Get a room." Everyone laughed and it took a couple of goes for the fat guy to get up as the floor was covered in body lotion, he kept slipping and ending up on Paula, it was brilliant.

The crowd cheered as the two of them went into the backroom to get changed and poor Paula was a mess god love her, her nicely done makeup was no more, her wee tight bun in her hair was gone and her hair now was like she was trailed through a hedge backwards and her tight fitting dress was up round her backside but she laughed it off and her mates got her another drink. As the house lights were turned off, the DJ started playing dance music again so everyone got on the dance floor and the party continued.

That night in the club was one of the busiest in a long time, we ran out of nearly everything and Billy was chuffed to bits at the takings, after everyone had left we pulled the shutter down and sat and had a pint, we decided to leave the clearing up until the next day as we were both knackered. As Billy lifted the shutter for us to leave, he was forced back into the club by two men with balaclavas on, he fell across the floor as one of the men shouted at me, "Where's the fucking money?" He pointed a gun at me, as he walked towards me, he shouted again, "Where's the fucking money?" I looked at Billy as he was just getting back to his feet. I noticed the other man had no gun and just as the one with the gun got up close to me, everything was so clear I could see exactly what I was going to do, it was like time had stood still in one instance I turned the lights off I grabbed the man's hand with the gun in it and smacked him such a smack in the face with my fist he fell to the ground screaming. The gun fell out of his hand and went off, it scared the crap out of me but I switched the lights back on again and grabbed the gun and pointed it at the now two men who were running out the door, I shouted after them, "If you come anywhere near here again I will blow the fucking heads off you."

They scarpered out the door and as I turned to Billy, he just stood there holding his head, there was blood running down the side of his face. I said to him, "Billy, Billy are you ok?"

As he felt his head he answered, "I think so Jonny, I must have hit my head when I fell."

I walked over to check him and thank goodness it was just a bump and a cut, I said to him, "Fuck Billy what just happened?"

He replied, "Jonny WHAT HAPPENED?! Holy shit, where did that come from I just remember the lights going out and then the gun going off what the fuck did you do?"

"I don't know what came over me Billy, I just snapped, but they won't be back."

"Jonny that was stupid, one of us could have been killed there."

"I know Billy I didn't think that far ahead." At that the realization of what could have happened hit me and I said to Billy, "I'm sorry Billy should I have just told them where the money was."

"Fuck no I'm glad you did hit him a smack and chased them out, the two dickheads probably would have shot one of us anyway, I will have to contact Sam and let him know what happened cause if that was the U.V.F then there will be trouble and Sam won't like it."

"Are you sure you want to go down that road Billy? We don't want a feud on the road, there is enough going on with this killer still running around."

"Aye you're probably right but you will need to dump that gun, god knows what it's been used for and you don't want to be caught in possession of it."

"You're right Billy, I will get rid of it tomorrow."

"No Jonny, get rid of it tonight, clean your prints of it and dump it in someone's bin on the way home."

"Aye ok Billy I'll do that."

We locked up and I got into my car, I drove

straight up to my kill room and measured out 10 feet from the front door and got a spade from my collection of tools and dug a hole. I cleaned the gun and placed it in a plastic bag and put it in the hole and covered it up, I thought I might need it someday so just best to hold on to it.

CHAPTER 16

Charged

I put what tools I needed in the van and locked up, on the drive down the road I got thinking about what had happened tonight, something changed in me again and I loved it. I now knew I wanted Jonty, not just to kill him but to have him strapped to my chair in my kill room and to watch him suffer.

When I arrived down home, a police car was waiting on me, I got out and as I walked over to the car a police man got out putting his hat on, when he walked towards me I knew something was wrong.

"Are you Jonny?" he asked.

"Yes," I replied, "What's up officer?"

"Jonny your house has been damaged." As I looked round at my wee house, the front windows were smashed and the door kicked in.

"Aw fir fuck sake," I replied as I walked over to the remains of the front door, the officer followed me as I went in and the living room was trashed, the TV was smashed to bits and the settee was slashed as well. I was raging, I turned to the officer and said, "Dirty bastards, look at the state of my house." As I walked round the mess I was really angry, I knew exactly who done it, the two fuckers that tried to rob the club so they must have knew me cause they know where I live.

The officer replied, "Terrible son, have you fell out with anyone recently?"

I could only give one answer, "No I haven't a clue."

"You will need to get them windows boarded up; should I phone a guy that does this sort of thing?"

"Aye that would be great," and then it crossed my mind, whoever did this did they go upstairs? Did they go into the loft and find my bag? I started panicking.

"How long will the guy be to fix the windows?" I asked.

The officer replied, "He will be here in an hour Jonny, is there anything else we can help you with?"

"No thanks I will get this tided up, thanks very much for your help."

"No worries Jonny, all in a day's work, just one last thing I have a message from Sergeant Porter."

My heart sunk. "Oh, what's that?" I asked.

"He told me to tell you, get it done."

I stood there numb and at that the officer walked over to the police car and got in, as he drove away I just stood there watching the red lights of the back of his car go down the street, as soon as it turned the corner I rushed into the house and I took the stairs 2 at a time. When I got to the top, I quickly looked round the two bedrooms, nothing had been touched, I lifted the chair from my mum's room and got up and looked up inside the loft. It was pitch black, I couldn't see a thing so I felt across and I gave a sigh of relief, my bag was still there, I opened it up and lifted out a handful of notes. I zipped the bag back up again and closed the lid, I got down and put the money in my pocket and put the chair back in my mum's room and closed the door, as I walked back down the stairs I looked round the living room and it was a mess. I started brushing up and lifting the broken ornaments and as I stood there in what was left of my wee house I felt really angry at who done this and if I ever found out who did it, they might just have a wee seat up in my kill room.

A van pulled up outside my house and it was the guy to fix the windows, as he got out of his van I walked out to meet him.

"Alright mate I take it you're here to fix this mess?"

"Aye I am." As he opened up the back of his van he looked up at the house, "Oh dear that's a bit of a mess, were you talking when you should have been listening?"

I looked at him, "No I wasn't whoever did this will pay if I find out, now can you fix it or do I have to get someone else?"

"Easy on there mate, I'm only joking."

"Sorry I am just annoyed about it," I replied

"It's alright, we will get it boarded up tonight and I will come back tomorrow and put you a couple of new windows in, but the door will be a week or so, so I will just have to try and patch it up for you."

"That's great thanks," I replied.

At that he lifted out a couple of boards and measured them to size then cut them, he nailed the first one on and then went and got the ladders off the roof of his van and lent them up against the side of the house. He asked me to hold them as he climbed up and boarded the other broken window up, he then came back down and took a look at the front door. He said to me, "This isn't too bad we can get away with a new lock so you won't need a new door."

"That's brilliant mate, thanks a lot."

He went into his van and lifted out a new lock, it took him about an hour in total but the house was now secure again. I asked him what time he would be back tomorrow and he replied about 3pm if that suited me, I said that would be great and off he went.

When I went back into the house, I just went on up to bed, it had been a really long day and as I looked at my watch it was bloody 4.30am. I closed my eyes and went to sleep.

It was near lunch time when I woke up and when I went down stairs I had to put the light on as with the window being boarded up, it was really dark. I made some breakfast and sat at the table, the house was really quiet not a sound, I could hear the odd car drive past but apart from that there was a real eerie feel about the place and I didn't like it, I looked at my watch and it read 1.15 so I decided I needed to go down the road and get a new TV and settee.

I went to the electrical shop on the Shankill and

bought myself a nice big TV and it wasn't too bad, 300 quid, and he even threw in the stand, pure bargain, I thought. I then went down to the furniture shop and I got an ex-display settee for a 150, so apart from the few ornaments which to be honest they done me a favour breaking them cause I never liked them anyway but couldn't face throwing them out, I was sorted. I even got the guy from the furniture shop when he was to deliver the new settee to take the ripped one away. I drove back up home and when I arrived, the window guy was there working away taking the broken windows out and replacing them with nice new white PVC ones, when he finished he gave me the bill which for boarding them up and then replacing them was 320 quid, I thought it was a bit of a rip off but when I looked at the job he done I was pleased so I just put a smile on and paid him.

I went down to work to help Billy get the bar sorted, but my thoughts were now on killing Jonty and I decided I would go and lift him that night.

When I arrived at work Billy wasn't there so I opened up and got started cleaning up, it wasn't until near opening time when Billy arrived. I said to him, "Billy what happened to you? I thought we were meeting at 5 to get sorted?"

He replied, "Jonny my car was done last night, the bastards burnt it out."

"Fuck Billy, my house was done as well they broke the windows and front door and trashed the place; do you think it was them bastards who tried to rob us last night?"

"I'm sure of it Jonny I will have to contact Sam to

see if he knows anything."

Just as Billy finished talking, Big Sam and Jonty walked in, I near dropped there and then I was raging, Jonty wasn't in Millisle. Sam spoke up, "I hear you had a bit of bother last night Billy?"

"Aye Sam we did, two men walked in one of them had a gun and tried to rob the place, if it wasn't for Jonny they would have got the heap."

I stood there looking at Jonty and noticed he was a bit swollen round his left eye, I looked really hard and the penny dropped, it was him who I had smacked last night, fucking Sam had set it up and yep that's how they knew where both Billy and I lived, dirty bastards, I thought.

Sam spoke again but this time he looked at me, "That was very stupid of you Jonny you should have just handed the money over." I knew by his tone he meant hand the money over to him and it maddened me inside, I was screaming and could see myself just killing the two of them there and then but on the outside, I was as cool as cucumber. I answered him, "Probably was Sam but Billy works too hard for scum bags just coming in thinking they can just take the money and just because they had a gun it doesn't mean they are untouchable." As I said that I looked at Jonty, he dropped his head.

I then looked back at Sam, he asked me, "So what did you do with the gun?"

"Dumped it, why do you ask?"

"Where did you dump it?"

"There was a load of bins out at the bottom of my

street, I put it in one of them but they were emptied today so it's gone."

"Pity I really wanted that gun," by Sam saying that I knew then it definitely was Jonty who was here last night, I looked at him again and thought to myself, that's the last straw, you are getting done tonight.

Billy spoke up, "So Sam what is going to be done about it, we can't have someone thinking that they can just walk in here with a gun and get away with it."

"Unless you can tell me who it is then there is nothing I can do, maybe if you donate a few quid each week to the loyalist fund then I could guarantee it won't happen again?"

"What, are you joking me Sam? You want me to start paying protection money when you and your team drink here for free? You are having a laugh."

"Billy don't take that tone with me if you don't be careful you will be closing that front door for good."

"Fir fuck sake Sam, there is no need for that."

"Then I can only see one outcome Billy, I need 100 a week from now on and I will collect it on a Monday when your delivery comes."

Billy just looked at me, he was white with rage but I knew there was nothing he could do, I said to him, "Billy just pay it, it's not worth the agro."

He never answered, I turned to Sam and said, "That's fine Sam we will pay it."

"See you boys on Monday then," Sam said as they walked out the door.

Billy walked over and pulled the shutter down he

walked back into the bar and was effing and blinding, he was furious, he turned to me. "That's a fucking joke, they are thieving bastards, there is no way I am paying them."

"Billy you will have to, they will close you down if you don't."

"Then they can close me down, I have had enough of this shit I will open up a bar somewhere else away from the Shankill."

"Billy don't be too hasty, something will turn up."

Billy walked away and poured himself a pint he looked over, "Jonny do you want one?"

I replied, "No Billy, I'm fine."

I wanted to be focused tonight and get that fucker and do him in.

All night I was trying to figure out how I was going to lift him and it wasn't until the darts match was over that I had a plan, I would just lift him from his flat down the road right out of his bed, it would be dangerous. I was running out of time so it had to be done tonight.

After work I drove up to get my van, I was very calm and relaxed, I was really looking forward to get him back to my room. As I parked my car round the back of the building, I took a minute and was wanting this over, Karen came into my head and I knew I wanted a life with her but had to finish this because I knew if Jonty and Sam was still about I couldn't have a life anywhere.

I got into my van and drove down home, I was too early to go and get Jonty, it had to be done in the early hours of the morning so I went to bed for a couple of hours, my dreams were all about Karen and getting a new life together away from the life I now have and maybe start a family of our own as I wasn't getting any younger and I'm sure Karen felt the same.

I had set my alarm for 4am and when I woke I was just busting to get going, I threw my clothes on and off I went, on the drive down the road it was really quiet, when I pulled into Jonty's street it was dark and really run down. A lot of the house were boarded up as it was planned for redevelopment, there was only a couple of houses that people still lived in and the block of 4 flats that Jonty lived in, he was the only one living there as it was to be knocked down as well. I pulled the van up along the flats and sat for a minute or so to make sure it was all clear and it was time, I got out and opened up the sliding door, I lifted out a balaclava and put it on, I then put a pair of gloves on and lifted the loaded gun I put it in my pocket. I lifted the sledge hammer and turned and walked towards Jonty's door, my heart was thumping, my adrenaline was in full flow, every foot step I got more excited. I got to his door and put my ear to it and listened, it was quiet, I tapped the glass slightly with my fist, I listened again. A light went on, it was a go, I swung the sledge hammer and smashed the door in. I pulled the gun out of my pocket and ran to where the light was, as I kicked the slightly opened door I pointed the gun at Jonty who was lying in his bed, I shouted at him, "Don't fucking move and get your hands where I can see them."

He lifted his hands out of the bed and his palms faced me, he said, "Don't shoot don't shoot, there is money in the drawer and there is a bag of drugs in there too just don't fucking shoot me take what you want."

"Oh I am taking what I want, now get out of bed."

Jonty started getting out of bed, he was just wearing a pair of shorts, he walked slowly towards me, I pointed the gun at his head.

"Where are you taking me?" he asked

"Just keep walking Ballbag," as he walked past me I put the gun to the back of his head, I pushed it in hard to make him walk faster and I walked him out to my waiting van. As I got to the open door I smacked him hard with the gun on the back of the head and pushed him in, he was out cold so I lifted the cable ties and got him tied up. I quickly looked round the street and one of the houses had their lights on, I hadn't much time, I knew they had heard me and probably had phoned the peelers. I slammed the door shut and ran round to the driver's side and got in, I started the van and sped off as I drove up the road I was buzzing, I got the bastard and now to have some fun watching him suffer.

I drove up the Ballygomartin Road and up the lane to my kill room, I turned the van and as I turned the key to turn the engine off, I could hear Jonty screaming in the back, he was kicking the door trying to escape, I laughed as I knew I had him and he was now at my mercy.

I got out and opened the big heavy door, I turned the light on and lifted my baseball bat, I walked slowly dragging the bat on the ground. When I got to the van, I tapped it a couple of times on the door, it went quiet, I had already removed my balaclava I wanted to see his face when I opened the door. As I opened the door expecting Jonty to be lying on the floor but no, as I pulled the door open he jumped out and on top of me, we both fell backwards and onto the muddy ground. He was trying to bite me and had headbutted me a couple of times before I managed to get him of me, I punched him a couple of times to the head and pushed him away from me, he still had his hands and feet tied so he couldn't go anywhere, he was screaming for help and I mean at the top of his voice and with it being the middle of the night and so quiet, his voice would carry for miles so I panicked and lifted the baseball bat and hit him round the head. His screams went silent as he lay there knocked out and blood coming out of his nose and mouth, I stood and listened, it was quiet, really quiet I turned and looked over Belfast, the view from up here at dawn was breath taking you could see right across to the ship yard in East Belfast and the hills of Hollywood were dark in the distance, it was very peaceful. Jonty started moving so I knew he was coming round, I grabbed both his feet and dragged him into the room and propped him up in the chair, he started moaning so I quickly cut the cable ties and strapped him into the chair before he realised what was going to happen. As I got the last strap fixed tight, he lifted his head and looked straight at me, I just stood there waiting for his reaction and then it came, "You bastard Jonny, it was you all along, Sam will cut your head off when he finds out."

"Don't worry Jonty, Sam will have his turn as well, if I was you I would be thinking how long I have got left to live."

"Jonny don't do this, you can let me go, you don't have to kill me, I swear I won't tell anyone." At that Jonty was sobbing, begging for his life but there was no way I could let him go, that would be as good as signing my own death warrant, so I turned and walked to my work bench. I lifted two 6 inch nails and a heavy hammer, I walked back over to Jonty and let him see the two nails, I said to him, "Just like old times Jonty, do you remember the night in the club with Gerrard and what you done to him? Well let's see how it feels."

"Jonny please, please don't, I was made to do it, I swear it was Sam, he made me," Jonty pleaded.

"Well Jonty you must have a really short memory 'cause I was there, you loved it and Sam had to tell you to stop."

"No Jonny you don't understand, I had to, please Jonny let me go, I can get you money, all the money you need."

At that he got my attention, "What do you mean; how much money?"

"Thousands Jonny, thousands, I know where Sam keeps it."

"Where Jonty, where does he keep it?" I asked.

"You have to let me go first, then I will tell you."

I knew he was lying, he was just trying to get me to drop my guard, I set one nail down and placed the other on Jonty's left foot, I lifted the hammer and hit it a heavy blow. The nail went straight through but it didn't go into the concrete floor, Jonty screamed in pain.

"Please Jonny, I will take you to his money, it's in a garage on the Shankill."

I lifted the other nail and placed it on his right foot, as I lifted the hammer I looked at him, I said, "Where is the money, what garage is it in?"

He hesitated so I brought the hammer down on the nail hard and it went straight through his foot but didn't go into the floor, he screamed again.

"It's at the bottom of Battenberg Street, the end garage," he sobbed out.

"Now that wasn't so hard was it Jonty?" I smirked at him.

"Are you going to let me go now Jonny?"

I didn't even answer him, I got up and walked over to the trolley of car batteries that I had set up and pulled them over to the side of Jonty's chair, he looked at them through the tears and said, "What the fuck Jonny? I told you what you wanted now you have to keep to your end of the deal."

"We didn't make a deal Jonty, I am not interested in Sam's money, I just want you to understand the pain that you inflicted on Gerrard and me and the hurt you caused to our families."

I lifted the set of jump leads and connected them to the row of batteries that were already connected together, I touched the black and red cable together and the sparks that came from them lit the room up. I did it again but this time I looked at Jonty, the fear in his eyes was brilliant, I could see the reflection of the sparks in his eyes, he was petrified, I bent down and connected the black lead to the nail on his left foot. I paused a second before connecting the red cable to the nail on his right foot, I wondered what would happen.

As I attached the red jump lead to the nail, it stuck to it like glue and Jonty started violently shaking, he was screaming. I stood back and just watched as foam started coming from his mouth, his eyes were bulging, he was in extreme pain, he pissed himself and the piss run right across the floor in front of me. I walked over and bent down to disconnect the red lead but I couldn't, it had welded itself to the nail. I tried to disconnect the black lead and it was the same, I stood up, smoke was now coming from Jonty's feet, the smell was horrific. I didn't want him dead yet so I went to the trolley of batteries and tried in vain to disconnect them but they were roasting hot, boiling in fact, I just pushed the trolley over as I thought they were going to explode, they fell with a crash and came apart. The connection was broken and Jonty slumped forward in his chair, the battery acid bubbled as it ran across the floor and the smoke was over powering, I choked as I ran for the door gasping for air and as I got to the door, the cool night air was a relief. As I filled my lungs with clean oxygen, I gave a couple of coughs and rubbed my eyes, as I turned and looked inside my room, the smoke was clearing and I could just see Jonty leant forward in the chair. I lifted a cloth from my van and put it over my mouth as I walked back in to check if Jonty was still alive.

As I got closer to him I recognised the smell, it was the same stench that haunted me for months, the smell of burning flesh, I knew then Jonty was dead. As I lifted his head, blood was coming from his eyes and his jaw dropped open and his tongue fell out onto his lap, he must have bit straight through it. He was dead, I was a bit disappointed as I wanted him to suffer more but the job was done. I lifted his tongue and walked over to my bench and opened up the jar with the other body parts in it, I dropped Jonty's tongue in and as it rested against Norman's ear and Jason's eye, I laughed as I said out loud, "Hear no evil, See no evil, Speak no evil," and laughed again when I said, "Paul you can give a hand to that," as his hand slowly settled beside all three.

I turned and looked at Jonty and the thought of Sam's money came to mind, I knew in that instant what I wanted to do.

CHAPTER 17

Sam's Money

As I stood there in my room, the stench was really strong, I decided my killing days were over. I wanted to make Sam suffer not just physically but mentally as well and for a long time, I went to my bench and lifted the last bullet, I lifted it up to the light and it shone like a star in the night sky, his name was etched into it, I decided to put it in the jar and keep it as a souvenir.

As I untied Jonty from his clasps, he was a pitiful site, he was still warm as I pulled him to the floor I lifted a rag and a bottle of water and washed the blood from his face. As I examined him further, his finger tips and toes were as black as coal, it was quiet sickening, I had to go outside for air and as I reached the front door I was sick I coughed and coughed and tears ran down my face. I got myself together and stood for a minute to think, I knew I couldn't take his body now to dump as it was too early in the morning, there would be too many people up and going to work it would be too risky, so I decided that I would have to leave him until tonight, it would give me time to find Sam's lockup.

I locked up and drove my van round the back, I got into my car and drove down home.

I had to get a shower before going to bed, I was not only covered in muck but as I stood in the shower scrubbing my skin I couldn't get the smell of burning flesh out of my nose, it was horrible it brought me right back to the time with Gerrard and the bar. I stood there with soap all over me and I cried, I must have cried for a good ten minutes and then I got myself together. I started remembering all the happy times in my life, my Christmas's with my mum and dad playing football for the school football team and winning the school's cup, working with Nigel on a Saturday and then Karen and oh, if I could only have gone back to the moment I met her how my life was so much easier then. As I stood there in the now freezing cold water I promised myself that I would do anything to get back with Karen and leave this life behind.

I rinsed the soap off me and turned the water off and got out and got dried, I went to bed and closed my eyes.

When I woke, I looked at my watch, it read 2.30pm. I got up and looked out the window, it was bucketing, the rain wasn't taking its time to come down, I felt sorry for the bin men who were round emptying the bins they were soaked to the skin and I smiled as it reminded me of the times working as a Saturday boy out on the lemonade run with Nigel and all the happy times I had then.

I got dressed and headed out the door to go down to Isabell's café for breakfast, I got my usual, a big ulster fry up and a mug of tea. As I sat by the window eating my breakfast, I watched the people going up and down the road going about their daily lives it was a busy wee road, as I mopped up the last of the egg yolk with the soda bread and horsed it into me, I took a big gulp of tea and finished my breakfast, I paid the bill and left to go and find Sam's lock up.

I drove down to the bottom of Battenberg Street and there was a row of 5 garages, I parked the car and got out to see which garage belonged to Sam as I examined the end garage on the left it was not even locked. I lifted the door and it was empty so I pulled the door back down and walked to the last garage on the right, as I got closer to it I noticed two big padlocks on it, when I bent down to examine them further the rain ran down the back of my neck and I shivered. I stood up and knew this was his lockup, I turned and looked round to make sure nobody had noticed what I was doing, I got back into my car and sat for a while just looking at the garage door and tried to figure out how I was going to break in with not too much noise, but most important was to replace the locks so the peelers wouldn't know I had been in and robbed Sam's money.

The only way round it was to replace the locks so that was what I had to do, I drove back down the road and called into the hardware shop and bought two locks that were as close to looking like the two I was going to cut off, I asked the guy behind the counter how I could get a lock off that I had lost the key to, he gave me a bolt cutter and showed me how to use it so I was set.

It was now 4.30pm and I had to get work, when I arrived Billy was just opening up.

"Alright Jonny, how's the form?"

"Filled in but not posted yet," I replied.

Billy laughed, "You're a laugh a minute Jonny boy, come on and we will get sorted, there is a band on tonight and they will be here shortly."

We walked into the bar and it was the usual routine, I restocked the bar as Billy cleaned up and we had a wee pint waiting on the band, when they arrived a few punters came in as well so it was time to start serving.

It was a younger crowd that night, hardly any of the regulars were in, the group was a two piece, a fella and a girl and they were pretty good but I knew we would have our work cut out for us 'cause they were drinking a lot of shots and vodka's. By 11pm, Billy had already had to split two fights up and buck them out, the group finished around 12 and it took us another hour to get the last of them out, my mind was running wild I couldn't wait till get down to Sam's garage and get his money.

I said goodnight to Billy and made the short walk to my car, there was a few drunks still hanging around trying to get taxis home, I got in and drove down to Battenberg Street where I parked the car with the boot right next to the door and got out. I opened the boot and lifted out the bolt cutters, I waited a second and just listened, no one was about so I bent down and *snip,* the first lock was of then *snip,* and the second fell to the ground. I held my breath as I lifted the door, it was pitch black, I couldn't see a thing so I decided to turn my ignition on in the car and put the reverse lights on, as I got back out of the car, the garage was light enough for me to have a hoke round. I plundered in a couple of boxes but they were just full of crap and then I noticed a big old wardrobe in the corner, I walked over and held my breath as I pulled the two big doors open.

Inside was two grip bags and as I lifted the first one, it was heavy, I slowly opened it up and it was full of notes, Jonty was right. I quickly closed it and threw it into the boot of my car, I didn't even check the next one I just put it in the boot as well and closed it, I pulled the garage door down and replaced the locks with the ones I had bought. I put the keys in my pocket and lifted the two cut locks and threw them over an awl fence and onto waste ground, I got into my car and drove up home. As I took the two bags into my living room, I sat them on the table, I turned the light on and closed the blinds.

I opened the first one and started lifting out bundles of money, there was a hell of a lot of money here and I knew in that instant that this was not just Sam's money, this was more than that, this was the U.F.Fs total fund and that scared me. I opened up the other bag and when I looked inside, it was full of guns and drugs, there was bags of tablets I mean thousands, this was trouble I shouldn't have taken it if I get caught with this I was a dead man. I zipped them up and brought them upstairs, I hid them under my ma's bed and went back downstairs and made a cup of tea, I sat there that night in my living room wondering what to do. I couldn't hand it over to the peelers and I certainly couldn't give it back to Sam and then there was Jonty still lying up the road in my room, my life was a mess and I was starting to lose control, it had to end.

I went back upstairs and lifted the bag with the drugs in it and put it into the boot of my car, I drove up to my kill room, there was only one thing I could do and that was to set Sam up, if I could do that I had a chance to get away.

I parked in the usual place and drove my van round the front to load Jonty's body in, as I opened the front door, the stench hit me, it was putrid. I coughed and coughed, I couldn't go in, it was too strong, I had to wait a while until the place got aired out. As I walked back in, I turned the light on and there lying on the floor was Jonty, he was lying in a pool of battery acid which had started to corrode his back and legs, as I walked over to him I turned him over with my foot. His back was white and wrinkled, parts of his skin were flapping around, it was disgusting, strips of his skin just fell off and then the smell hit me again, tears ran down my face as I coughed and gasped for air. I started feeling really dizzy and I staggered to the door, everything was blurry and I felt really sick, I threw up and had to sit down, I sat there looking over Belfast with my head in my hands just sitting in my own thoughts and concentrating to breathe. The sickness and dizziness left me and I started feeling a bit better, I looked back into the room and knew I had to get Jonty's body out and into my van. I went into the back of my van and lifted a rag and tied it round my mouth and nose, I held my breath and went back into the room, I grabbed Jonty by the feet and trailed him outside. I removed the rag and exhaled, I lifted Jonty again by the feet and trailed him into the back of the van and left him lying in a heap, I slammed the door shut and walked back into my room where I turned the light off and as I locked the door the rain started coming on again. I jumped into the driver's seat and put the keys into the ignition, as I was just about to start the engine, my hands started stinging, as I turned them over to look at my palms they going red in front of my eyes. I jumped out and put them into a puddle, it seemed to cool them down but when I looked at them again, they started stinging again they were on fire, I quickly put them back in the puddle and lifted a handful of muck and rubbed them together, that seemed to do the trick so I quickly rubbed them in the long wet grass and dried them on my jeans. I got in and started the drive back down to Battenberg Street.

The windows started steaming up so I put the heater on and on full blast the motor squealed and started blowing. "Bollix," I said as I opened up my window to try and get the window cleared, but it wasn't helping, the rain was now getting heavier and I leaned forward and wiped part of the window so I could see out. I squinted as I kept leaning forward trying to see the road I was glad to get onto the Ballygomartin Road, with the street lights on, I could see a bit better.

I drove down past the Woodvale Park and onto the Shankill Road a few streets down and I turned right into Battenberg Street, as I got to the bottom of the street I positioned my van so the sliding door was up against the Garage door. I turned my engine off and got out, I walked round to get the garage door open, the rain was now bouncing and I was getting wetter and wetter, I just about had enough room to lift the door and it acted as a roof. When I opened up the sliding door of my van, I grabbed Jonty by the arms and trailed his limp body into Sam's garage. I propped him up against one of the side walls and when I stood back and looked at him, the battery acid had started to work on his face and chest, they were now white and wrinkled and he looked like something out of a horror film. It was an appropriate look for him to have when they found him as he was a monster in real life and deserved nothing less.

I lifted the bag of guns and drugs and put them back into the wardrobe and closed the door over, I walked back outside and pulled the garage door shut. I quietly closed the sliding door of my van and got in and drove off, I had only one more job to do and that was destroy my van and kill room.

I arrived back up and parked the van just by my car and got in and drove my car down the lane a bit. I parked it up and I slowly walked back up the lane, I was dragging my feet, I was exhausted. As I opened up the room and turned the light on, I started to remove anything I wanted to keep, when I got to the pickled egg jar I lifted it and just stared inside, the body parts floated round and as I looked closer, I swear the eye just looked straight through me, it was like it was judging me. My grip loosened and I dropped the bloody thing, it smashed on the ground at my feet and I jumped back as it did, I said, "Well that's that then, you're getting burnt as well."

I kicked them over and into the battery acid where they started bubbling, I lifted my tools from the bench and put them in a grip bag, I left them outside. As I walked back over to the chair I lifted my right foot and using the sole of my shoe, I kicked the chair a couple of times until it broke free from the bolts that I had used to secure it to the floor and kicked it over to my nanny's furniture that lay in the corner. I then walked over and lifted one of the containers of petrol that I had bought and started sprinkling it over everything in the room, I especially poured plenty over the batteries, I knew once they started burning they would keep the fire going.

I went out and drove my van against the door just leaving enough room just to squeeze by, I then lifted the other container of petrol and sprinkled it all round the inside of the back of the van and then all over the seats. I used all of it and then threw the container back into my room, the smell of petrol was really strong so I knew once I struck the match I had to get off side really quickly.

I planned the best way to light it and then lifted the box of matches out of my pocket, I stood back and struck the match. I covered it with my other hand to stop the rain from putting it out and I watched as it burned down a bit, it was really peaceful just standing there watching that match and just as it was getting close to burn my finger and thumb I threw it into my room and *whoosh!*

It took hold, I watched for a brief moment as the flames moved across the floor lighting everything in its path, I lifted another match and struck it. I threw it into the inside of the front of my van and again the flames engulfed it, I slowly walked backwards just watching my van and room go into a huge inferno. I knew I hadn't much time before the fire brigade would be alerted, I ran down the lane to my car and got in and sped off, as I looked in my rear view mirror, the flames must have been 20 foot high. As I got onto the Ballygomartin Road I remembered I hadn't lifted my bag of tools, I hit the steering wheel and said, "Fuck, fuck, fuck." I just hoped the fire would destroy them, there was nothing I could do now as when I pulled round the corner of the Woodvale Park, a fire engine with its lights and horn blasting drove past me and as I drove onto the Shankill, a peeler car flew past me as well. I drove into my street and parked up, I gave a sigh of relief as I knew I was finished, my killing days were over and it was like a huge relief lifted off my shoulders.

I locked my car and opened up my front door, I walked straight into the kitchen and put the kettle on and a couple of rounds of bread under the toaster. When they were ready I slapped plenty of butter on and set them on a plate, I lifted a tea bag and made a cuppa, I then went and sat in the living room and by God that tea and toast was the nicest tea and toast I had ever tasted. When I finished I left my cup and plate in the sink and went on up to bed.

I lay all night tossing and turning, everything was going through my head, I couldn't sleep a wink and by 6am I was up again and downstairs. I needed to know if all the evidence was destroyed and then there was Sam, I needed to finish it and phone the confidential police phone number and tell them about his garage but I had to pick my moment, I couldn't leave it too late as Jonty's body would be decomposing, especially that it was covered in battery acid the process would be quicker.

Billy had given me the day off which I was glad, I needed some time alone to plan how this would finish, I needed to speak to Porter to see if he knew anything about the fire and to see if they had found any evidence that could tie me to the scene so by 10am I decided to give him a ring.

"Hello Porter I need to speak with you."

"Hello Jonny, have you any news for me anything of interest?"

"I haven't seen Sam now for a couple of days, I think he is in hiding somewhere but I don't feel safe, I need out," I replied.

"Jonny unless we have concrete evidence that can connect Sam to his illegal going ons, then I'm sorry son you're on your own."

"We had a deal Porter, you told me if I didn't feel safe your team would pull me out so don't back out now," I said angrily.

"Things have changed son, I told you before we need him off the road so it's up to you how you do it and that's the only deal there is."

I hung up on him, I threw the phone on the settee, I was fuming, typical peeler just used me but I still had the upper hand. I walked upstairs and started counting Sam's money, I put the bundles of notes out in piles of 500 quid and when I had them all stacked, it came to 70,000 quid so I had enough to buy a new life somewhere else but it could only be possible if Karen would go with me.

I put the money back in the bag and went upstairs and hid it under my ma's bed.

I drove over to the Falls Road and found a payphone, as I dialled the number of the confidential police number, my heart was racing, this was it, this was the day I had planned for a long time as I dialled the final digit I waited for an answer and then it came.

"You are through to the police confidential line, how can I help you?"

It was a girl on the other line, I panicked a bit I just said, "I need to speak to someone about a murder."

"You can speak with me, what is the information?"

I could hear her typing on the other end of the line, I repeated to her, "Do you hear me; I need to speak to someone about a murder?"

"Yes I do but you need to tell me the information you have before I can pass it on to the appropriate department so they can act on it."

I took a breath and said to her, "There is a garage at the bottom of Battenberg Street, the end one on the right, it belongs to Sam Colins, he runs the Shankill, you need to look inside."

I hung the phone up, that was it, it was done I couldn't go back now, it was a waiting game and I needed to keep a low profile so I drove up home and just closed the blinds and sat and watched the TV.

I sat for an hour or so but it was eating away at

me, I needed to know if the police had reacted to the information I gave them, so I decided to take a drive down, as I drove out onto the Shankill and up to Battenberg Street I slowed down. I looked down the street, it was clear, my heart sunk, I drove up to the next street and turned down it, it ran parallel to Battenberg Street so I was able to drive right down to the bottom of it and straight past the garages, the street was empty, the garage hadn't been touched there was something wrong but I couldn't figure out what.

I drove back up home to get the phone to ring Porter, he must know what's going on, I sat in my living room and rang him, he didn't answer so I rang again and again and again it took about 10 goes before he answered.

"Jonny I can't talk, there has been a development, I will ring you later."

And he hung up, I knew then that they had got the information and they were putting a plan together. "Yes," I said as I punched my fist in the air. "They are going to get him." I was chuffed to bits, I needed to get offside in case Sam got wind of what was going to happen so I decided to go over to East Belfast and take a walk round Conswater shopping centre with it being a Sunday, there would be loads of people so it would be safe to spend a couple of hours.

CHAPTER 18

Eye To Eye

As I drove down the Shankill my stomach told me it was lunch time but I didn't want to take the chance on going to my usual café so I drove over to the Newtownards Road and parked outside a café on the corner of Dee Street. As I walked in the door, it felt like everyone in the place was staring at me, I sat down by the window and just buried my head in the menu, after a couple of minutes a girl came over to take my order. "Can I get you something to eat?" she asked.

As I lifted my head I replied, "Yeah could I have a fry and a cup of tea please?"

"Certainly love it won't be long," she replied as she turned and walked away, I looked round and noticed a table over in the corner with newspapers on it, I walked over and lifted the Sunday World as I sat back down I looked at the front page and there was Sam and Jonty right there the front page. The blood drained from me, the headlines read; *'Sam Colins U.F.F commander up to his neck in drugs, prostitution and money laundering. His side kick Jonty has also been reported missing and suspected on the run from an internal Feud.'*

Brilliant, I thought, the papers are saying all the right things, it puts Sam in the frame, I turned to page six where the whole story was being told, I only got about half way through when the girl came back with my fry. I looked up and thanked her but I couldn't enjoy it, I was more interested in what the papers had to say about Sam.

After I finished reading, I tucked into the rest of my fry and as I sat drinking my tea I knew then why I hadn't seen Sam about, he was in hiding alright and I knew where.

I had to tell Porter, I paid my bill and got into my car, I lifted the phone and rang Porter he answered straight away, "I told you Jonny, I can't speak."

I answered straight away, "It's about Sam, I know where he is."

"Where Jonny, where?"

"Oh so I have your attention then?" I replied with a smirk on my face.

"Just fucking tell me where he is," Porter was furious.

"Hold on Porter I need to know where I stand before I tell you, I need assurances you aren't going to hang me out to dry."

"Ok Jonny, ok, anything just tell me where he is."

"I need it in writing that no charges are to be used against me and if you want the information meet me in the Park Avenue hotel car park in an hour."

I hung the phone up before he could answer, he tried ringing me back a couple of times but I never answered.

I took a walk round the shops in Conswater shopping centre and with about 10 minutes to spare, I drove up the Hollywood Road and into the car park at the Park Avenue Hotel, as I drove in there was a big black car sitting away over in the corner on its own, it flashed it's lights so I knew it was Porter. I parked alongside it with my driver's window right up against its driver's window, as I looked in through the tinted glass I could see two men sitting in suits, one of them was Porter, I wound my window down as they did. I said, "Have you something for me?"

I was handed an envelope, the driver said as he still held on to it, "Have you something for us?"

"I want to check this first." As I snatched it out of his grip, I opened it up it looked official with a police stamp on it, I read through it, and it was perfect.

"One thing Porter, I want you to sign this?"

As I handed it back, Porter looked at me and said, "What's wrong Jonny, do you not trust me?"

I replied, "Do I fuck, just sign it."

He lifted a pen from his inside pocket and signed it and handed back over to me, he said, "Are you Happy now? Just tell me where Sam is."

"He's in Millisle, they have a house down there, the street beside the bar it's the 2nd house on the left going down."

At that they sped off, I sat and read the piece of

paper again just to make sure it was air tight, I wondered what would happen if it got destroyed, I would be back to square one and be the peelers puppet again.

I knew then I had to protect myself if anything was to happen, I drove up home and decided I had to get my money out of the house and hide somewhere safe. I wrecked my brains and the only place I could come up with was a locker down at the bus station so that's what I did, I had to get two lockers as I could only fit Sam's bag in the first one so I put my kit bag in the one beside his but not before I took a couple of grand out for pocket money. I locked them up and got back into my car and drove up home.

I hid the keys in a vase that sat in the window and memorised the numbers, 141 and 142, it was near perfect, the only thing now was to get a solicitor and leave the letter with them, but I had to pick a high profile solicitor that would stand against the peelers and not sell me out.

The next morning, I drove into town, I drove round and round and it wasn't until the third time going down Queen Street that I noticed a solicitors that specialised in criminal law, it was called Rice and Co. I think I saw them on TV representing a member of the I.R.A and that they won the case on a technicality, so I thought, they are the firm for me.

I parked the car and walked over, as I entered the building the girl behind the desk smiled and said, "Can I help you sir?"

"Yes I need to speak to someone regarding a possible prosecution."

"That's not a problem, take a seat and I will get someone to speak to you straight away."

"Thanks." I turned and sat down in what was the comfiest leather seat, I sunk right into it if I didn't know better I would have closed my eyes and just fell asleep, it was heaven.

"Hello can I help you?"

Shit I had closed my eyes, I woke up with a jerk, I stood up, in front of me stood a girl not much older than me dressed to kill, I might add in a two piece suit and nice white blouse. She was very distinguished her black hair tied back in a ponytail and black framed glasses, it made her look really important.

"Sorry about that, your chair was really comfy and I am knackered, haven't done much sleeping lately." I could feel my face burn as I spoke.

"You're ok, follow me and we will speak somewhere private," she turned and started walking away, my eyes where fixated on her bum, oh my God she had some wiggle, if nothing else I would come back just to see that bum, I followed her into a small room just down the corridor and sat down opposite her at a table.

"We will make a start, what is your name?"

"Jonny Andrews."

"Ok Jonny, my name is Teresa and I am a partner here at Rice and Co. now what seems to be the problem?"

"I need to know anything we talk about here is confidential and that anything I give you will be kept safe and if I get arrested that you will fight my corner?"

"Slow down Jonny, that is a lot to take on board, are you in some sort of trouble?"

I explained the whole situation, Porter and the deal we had, I just left out the wee bit about killing Sam's crew and setting Sam up, I just told her I was an informant and that Porter had given me a letter so that I was a free man, I handed Teresa the letter and she looked it over.

"This is quite something Jonny, I'm glad you came to me with it as this is a form of collusion and is a massive piece of evidence we can use against the police."

"Woah, hold on, you aren't to use this unless I get arrested and you can only use it to get me out of jail, you aren't to use it for anything else."

"Well if that is the case Jonny, it will cost you."

I knew this was coming. "How much?" I replied.

"For holding information and for possibly representing you with this sort of information, you're talking in the region of 1000 pounds and if there is a case put against you and we have to go to the crown court that will extensively rise and if you lose then you could be talking 10s of thousands."

"Are you serious? But with this letter surely the peelers wouldn't have a case against me?"

"Yes that's all well and good but I have never seen a letter like this before so I don't know if it will stand up in court."

"Look all I want you to do is keep it locked up safe and if I get arrested then you produce it and as long as I am released then it's yours to do with whatever you want."

"Ok Jonny then I would need a payment of 200 pounds just to hold this until you let us know when to use it."

At that I went into my pocket and lifted a wad of notes out, I counted 200 and handed it to her.

"Can I have a receipt for that and a contact number for you?"

Teresa took the money and said, "Yes Jonny that's not a problem, just wait here I will be back in a moment."

Teresa left the room; it gave me time to catch my breath I couldn't believe I was doing this, life was so complicated and I hoped I was near the end and just wanted to run away from it all.

After about 10 minutes Teresa returned, she sat down again. "Jonny I was talking your case over with a colleague and we are glad to be representing you and that there won't be a charge as long as you agree that we can produce your letter in open court even if you don't get arrested."

"No I can't agree to that, if you do that I'm a dead man, again you can only use it for me if the police arrest me and that is all I want."

"So after we produce it in court to say that you were working for the police and that they had agreed not to press charges, are you not going to be in danger then?"

"Let me deal with that, I don't plan to be around it's just in case the police go back on their word."

"Then that's fine Jonny."

At that Teresa stood up and shook my hand, she gave me a business card with her telephone number on it and said, "I wait for your call Jonny."

"Hopefully not Teresa," at that I thanked her and left.

I drove back up the Shankill and couldn't resist the fry in Isabell's café so I pulled over outside and went in.

I sat there eating my fry, unconcerned as you like and as I was just eating the last of my soda bread, I heard a familiar voice, "Hello Jonny I believe you have been a busy boy."

I knew that voice, my heart missed a beat, I looked up, it seemed to take forever but there in front of me was Sam, I couldn't breathe, my heart was thumping, I went to speak but nothing came out.

"What's wrong Jonny cat got your tongue?"

I coughed, "No Sam, what's up?"

"I have been looking for Jonty but nobody seems to know where he is, have you any idea where he is?"

I stuttered, "No Sam, I don't."

"I have been keeping a close eye on you Jonny and I think it's time you stepped up to the mark and got more involved with the business."

I couldn't believe what I was hearing, at first I thought I was going to be shot but he didn't have a clue, I didn't know what to say, a few other people that were in the café looked round. Sam then said, "Can you all leave? I need a bit of privacy."

Not one person questioned him, they all just got up and left, even the two girls that were serving left as well. I started panicking, I could feel my hands shake, I stood up.

"Sit down Jonny, I only want to give you a proposition, you don't have to give me an answer straight away."

At that Sam sat down opposite me. "Jonny I am really worried about Jonty, he is not answering his phone and his family don't know where he is, now I know you and him didn't see eye to eye but have you heard anything about where he could be?"

I paused a minute before I answered, "Sam I haven't seen Jonty in days, I thought you and him were away somewhere keeping a low profile."

"No Jonny we weren't and I am getting worried where he is."

"I'm sure he will turn up, you know what he is like, he is probably shacked up with some bird and will turn up wondering what all the fuss has been about." I just stared at Sam hoping he would buy it.

"I'm sure you're right Jonny but more importantly I need you getting more involved with our team and more hands on if you know what I mean?"

"I do know what you mean Sam, I will need more time to think about it."

"That's fine Jonny but I will need an answer by tomorrow."

"Ok Sam call in to the club tomorrow night and I will let you know then."

Sam got out and walked outside just leaving me sitting there; I gave a sigh of relief and took a drink of tea.

I heard the screeching of tires and a lot of shouting, I stood up and looked outside and to my amazement there were 3 peeler cars blocking the road and about 6 peelers with guns all pointing at Sam. I saw Porter standing there, I don't think he saw me, I just stood there and watched as one peeler walked forward shouting at Sam to get down and put his hands on his head. I watched Sam as he stood there not knowing what to do, he was pointing and shouting calling the peelers all the black bastards under the sun, when the peeler got over to Sam, he pushed him and told him to get to the ground. He obviously didn't do his homework, as soon as he pushed Sam, Sam swung a right hook and knocked the peeler to the ground, four other peelers rushed in and wrestled Sam to the ground, all hell broke loose as people were standing watching and Sam screaming and shouting. Just then a police van pulled up and they grabbed Sam and threw him inside, I stood there numb but I watched Porter and I wanted to see what he was doing.

He stood watching the people that had gathered and when the last peeler got into the last car, he looked straight over at me, we exchanged a glance as I watched back he stood there in his long black over coat and just nodded once and got in to the awaiting car and drove off.

It was like time was on slow motion, what had just happened? Is it over? Is that it? Was I free?

All these questions were going through my head, what was I to do now?

CHAPTER 19

It Could Have Been Me

I left the café and drove up the Shankill, I turned left into Battenberg Street the suspense was killing me. I needed to know if the peelers were at Sam's garage and when I got about half way down the street, it was cordoned off with white tape and a police man was in the middle of the road. I pulled over and got out of my car, as I walked over to the peeler I could see down the bottom of the street and there were men in white boiler suits and they were in Sam's garage, so I knew they had found Jonty and hopefully the bag of guns and drugs so Sam would be jailed for a long time. As I got up to the peeler, I said, "What's happening down there?" as if I didn't know.

The peeler replied, "I'm sorry sir I can't divulge that information, you will have to turn your car and find different route."

As I looked past the peeler and down the street, I saw a body bag being lifted out of the garage, I said to the peeler, "Is that a body they have taken out of there?" and I pointed down the street.

The peeler turned round and then back again, "It looks very like sir, now can you be on your way?"

I replied, "Yeah no worries mate." I smiled as I turned and got into my car, I did a three point turn and drove back up and onto the Shankill, as I drove up home I had the window down and the music blasting, life was good, I knew everything was going to be ok and for the first time in a long time I was happy.

I got into the house and got ready for work, I had a quick cup of tea and tided up a bit before heading for work at 4pm.

When I got down, the delivery lorry pulled in behind me and Billy came walking out of the bar.

"Alright Jonny, good timing, it's a big order today as we have a couple of charity do's this week."

"No worries Billy," I replied as I started lifting crates of beer in.

"What's the crack Billy?" I asked as Billy lifted the bottles of WKD in.

"Did you hear about Sam?" Billy asked.

"Aye Billy they took him down right on the Shankill, I hear they took a body out of his garage as well."

"Fuck Jonny he will go away for his tea for sure now."

"I know Billy thank fuck, I'm glad they lifted him, he wanted me to join his team."

"No way Jonny, did he ask you himself?"

"Aye Billy, right before they lifted him."

"Fuck I'm sure you are glad then, you don't want to get involved in all that especially now they have lifted him, if you were involved they probably would scoop you as well."

"I know Billy, it couldn't have come at a better time."

I lifted another couple of crates of beer and walked into the club, about another hour of hawking in the order and I was wrecked. I sat for a while with a tin of *Coke* and Billy went down and got some chips in. We sat there and just chatted about Sam and wondered with him out of the way who would take over the road and to be honest it didn't matter who it was anybody would be better than Sam.

We ate our chips and drank our *Coke* and got the bar set up for the pool team arriving.

It was just like old times, the whole atmosphere had changed and the crack was flying, it was a really good night and even though the pool team lost we had a really good night and even had time at the end of the night for a few beers as well.

As Billy locked up, I decided since I had had few drinks just to walk down home and it was a nice night so the dander would do me good, I said goodbye to Billy and started the walk home.

As I turned the corner in my street, a car drove slowly past me, I looked in it but didn't recognise the two guys. My heart got faster as I knew something was going to happen, I started walking a bit faster trying to get into the safety of my house but as I got about ten feet from my front door, a man with a balaclava on came out of the alleyway and stood there in front of me. The car pulled up alongside the kerb and another man got out, I took to my heels to run but one of them grabbed me, he wrestled me to the back of the car and the other man had the boot open. I started to shout for help but it was too late, they threw me in to the boot and slammed it, I heard the doors slam shut and the car sped off.

It was so dark in that boot, but I knew what was ahead of me so I had to get a plan and I knew it was them or me. As the car went round a few corners, I shifted side to side, I felt into the back of my trousers for the gun that I now always carried and it was a case of keeping calm and I had to just wait for the boot to open up again.

It must have been a good twenty minutes before eventually the car stopped, this was it, I shuffled round so my feet were going to be to the open boot and I raised the gun and waited, I held my breath as I heard the car doors open and footsteps as they walked to the back of the car, I cocked the gun and as I heard one of them say, "Let's do this wee bastard, he deserves what is coming to him."

The boot opened, my heart was pounding but soon as the first round went off, I was so calm. *Bang*, right in the chest, I could see another one turn to run and *bang* right between the shoulder blades and he fell to the ground. I leant forward and looked out of the boot and the other one was running away, I got out of the boot and stood over the two men lying in the dirt, I pointed the gun at the first one's head and pulled the trigger, his head moved to the side as the bullet struck it and the rush that I got was amazing. I pointed the gun at the man that was now trying to crawl away, he turned on to his back and pleaded with me not to shoot him but he was talking to the wrong guy and *bang* right through his forehead, his brains just splattered on the muck beneath him, he was dead. I looked up and I could just see the third man duck in to an outbuilding, I slowly walked towards him with the gun pointed towards where he had hid.

As I got closer, I could hear him breathe, I stopped for a minute and just listened, I could hear him breathe really heavy he must of known I was outside. I said, "We can do this the easy way or the hard way, it's up to you mate, now don't make me come in there, why don't you come out and we can talk about this?"

He answered, "You're going to kill me, I don't want to die."

"As long as you tell me what I want to know, you can walk away from this."

"Can I have your word?" he replied, I could hear him crying.

"Yes now just come out with your hands in the air."

I stood back with the gun pointed at the open door and waited, a figure emerged and with the moon light I could just see him with his hands in the air, he pleaded, "Don't shoot me, I didn't know they were going to kill you I swear."

"Calm down, I only want to talk to you, now come out and get on your knees with your hands behind your head."

He did what I asked and as I walked over behind him putting the gun to the back of his head and feeling down round his waist for a gun, he was clean. I walked round to face him and as I did I noticed tears running down his cheeks, he looked really young, about 17 or so, he was in bits. As I stood in front of him he looked up at me, "Please Mr, don't kill me, I was only meant to drive the car I didn't want to do this but they made me."

It reminded me of the time up at Belfast Castle so I knew exactly how he was feeling, I said to him, "Who sent you and what do you know?"

"It was Sam, he sent us, it was him," he was really in a panic.

I told him, "Calm down, now what's your name?"

"It's Calum, I didn't want to be part of this but they made me," he repeated.

I stood there, I felt sorry for the lad but I had a decision to make, put one in his head or let him go.

I paused a minute and then I said to him, "What age are you Calum and where do you live?"

"I'm 18 and I live in Shankill estate, I swear Mr they made me come, they said it was just a beating, that you were a house breaker."

I believed him, it was one of the ways Sam would get young lads involved. "Right so this is how it is, I'm not going to kill you yet but if you go to the peelers then I will come to Shankill estate and find where you live and burn you and your family in your beds, do you understand me Calum from Shankill estate?"

"I do Mr, I do," he replied really sobbing.

"Then get up and be on your way."

Calum got up and started walking away, I stood and watched him as he got about 20 feet away and then just as I was about to turn away, he caught my eye as he bent down and lifted a gun from his right leg, as he turned to face me and just and as he raised the gun he shouted, "Die tout."

He didn't stand a chance, before he even got to pull the trigger I had two in his chest, he fell backwards and onto the road I walked slowly over to him where he was gasping for air. I got down on one knee beside him, he was coughing as blood run from his mouth, his eyes were wide open and I had seen that fear before as a man was about to die. I said to him, "Calum why son? Why didn't you just go home?"

He coughed again and then went silent, he died right there in front of me and to be honest I felt really sad at such a waste of life and again even though that bastard Sam was locked away, he still had boys doing his dirty work. I knew then I should have killed him and that I would always be looking over my shoulder for the next one to come.

I got into the car that they had used and turned it round and drove down the road, I hadn't a clue where I was until I saw the sign for Belfast. I think I was up round Mullusk somewhere so as I got onto the motorway, I headed for home but I knew I had to ditch the car somewhere, so I went to an old favourite spot up near Glencairn estate and as I parked the car I lifted some rubbish that was in the hedge row and put it in the front seat and lit it. I waited until I made sure it was well alight and then walked off, as I got about 100 yards away, the car exploded. I jumped as it went off but I knew that there would be no trace of me being in it.

It took me about 20 minutes to walk down home and I couldn't get Calum out of my head, I felt it for his family but suppose it could have been me.

CHAPTER 20

On The Run

———·◊·——————————·◊·———

When I got back home and into the safety of my living room, I sat for a while and thought about what had just happened. Sam must know I was working for the peelers and he wouldn't stop until he killed me, so I knew I wouldn't have much time left before he would try again but to be honest, I enjoyed the power again and feared now at what I had become.

I sat looking round my house and knew I would have to leave it all behind if I was to escape the life I now was living, I went and got washed and again put my clothes in a bin bag to be dumped the next day and went to bed.

The next morning when I woke, I had a lot to do but first, get the TV on and see what was on the news; it wasn't long before a bulletin came on and the girl on the TV started reporting, "Three bodies have been found on waste ground at Mullusk, it is suspected that it was a drug deal went wrong and that the police are looking into a possible feud between loyalist fractions," and again the same routine if anyone had any information to contact the police, and then a telephone number came across the bottom of the screen.

Yes, I thought, well done Porter, you really are thick as champ and again I was in the clear, but then as I looked over at my bag of clothes, the realisation that Sam would know that there was only one person who could have killed the three of them, ME.

I made some breakfast and then packed a bag, I took one last look round the house and as I closed the front door behind me for the last time, I had only one thing on my mind, a new life somewhere far away, but I really wanted to see Karen one last time before I would disappear. I only had two days left to organise it and that was now my focus, my plan was to meet Karen on Thursday night and try and explain this whole nightmare, I would ask her to come with me but to be honest if I was her, I would never want to see me again, never mind run away with me.

I opened the boot of my car and threw my bag in along with the bag of clothes that I had to dump, I drove down to Agnes Street and parked the car, I lifted the bag of clothes out and threw it in to one of the skips in the council yard. It was very busy so I knew it would never be found and walked back to the car, as I drove down the Shankill, it brought back so many memories, walking up and down the road with my ma buying carpet and wallpaper with her, going into town with her and getting my first pair of boots. I then drove past the memorial to the Shankill bomb which angered me as that was a turning point in my life where things changed forever and then driving past Dover street where I used to meet Nigel selling the Maine lemonade, I drove into Belfast and over to the bus station where I had to pick my money up.

As I parked my car and got out, a police car came flying past with its sirens blasting, it made me feel really uncomfortable but I walked on into the depo and over to the lockers. As I stood in front of my two, I made the decision to just take one bag, so number 142 would stay as safe keeping for another time.

I drove on up towards Shaftsbury Square and on up Botanic, I pulled into one of the side streets and parked the car. I lifted both my bags out of the boot and wandered over to a local hotel, I went into reception to book a room and the girl was really nice and gave me a room overlooking the main road.

As I stood there looking out onto the busy road, Billy came into my mind, I didn't want to just leave without saying goodbye, he had been really good to me over the years and to be honest he was more of a dad to me then a boss. it would be hard but I had to give him a ring and explain, I knew I couldn't go and see him as Sam would have someone watching the club for me and I knew there was a bullet out there with my name on it.

I lifted my mobile out of my bag and dialled the club's number, it didn't take too long for Billy to answer, "Hello Heather Street social club, Billy speaking, can I help you?"

"Hello Billy, it's Jonny."

"Fuck sake Jonny, are you ok? It's all over the road that Sam is looking for you, what has happened?"

"Billy I can't tell you, I wish I could but too much has happened, I am just letting you know I won't be back on the Shankill, I have to leave Norn Ireland."

"Hold on Jonny, we can get this sorted, Sam is inside and it looks like they are charging him with murder as well as running an illegal organisation so he will be going away for a very long time."

"Billy you don't understand, I have to leave, Sam won't stop until I am dead there is only one thing I can do and it is run."

"Jonny son don't run, you have to face up to him, if you go now then you will be looking over your shoulder your whole life."

"I know Billy, it's a chance I will have to take, listen to me Billy, if I don't make it I have left something for you it's a bag and it's in a locker in the bus station in town, number 142. Now there is instructions in it and you have to promise me you will carry them out."

"Jonny, what do you mean?"

"Exactly what I just said, the instructions are in the bag, I have left a copy of the key in the store room under the *Coke* tins but promise me don't tell anyone, it's not safe anymore Billy, you can't trust anyone."

"I will Jonny, I promise you, is this it Jonny, is this goodbye?"

"Yes Billy it is, I wish it could be any other way but it can't, I really will miss you Billy but I have to disappear, I will check in with you after a while but it will only be a phone call."

I couldn't talk anymore, I was really cut up about

saying goodbye, I had to hang up so I just stood there in that lonely room looking out over the road and a tear trickled down my cheek. I was a mess, I hated having to say goodbye but it had to be done, if I stayed I was dead.

As I looked out the window, I noticed a barber's and when I looked in the mirror that was hanging on the wall, I really had let myself go, it was time to get sorted and be a man.

I lifted a few quid out of my bag and left the hotel, I walked across the busy road and into the shop there was a young lad on the desk. "In for a trim mate?" he asked.

"Yes I am, a tidy up and a shave."

"No worries, take a seat and one of the guys will take you shortly."

I sat down and just watched as the two Barbers were busy cutting hair, they really were very good at their job, it wasn't long before it was my turn, I sat in the chair and the young fella asked me, "What would you like done mate?"

"Aw, just a tidy up and could I get shaved as well?"

"Yeah no worries mate."

It was really relaxing getting my hair cut and then shaved, he even gave me a head, neck and face massage, it was brilliant. I had to look twice in the mirror as I hadn't seen this fella in a long time, I tipped him an extra couple of quid and I left feeling good about myself.

I walked down the road a bit and into a man's clothes shop, I spotted a lovely pair of jeans. a really nice white shirt and even treated myself to new shoes and boxers. it felt great just able to buy nice things and not needing to worry about the cost. I called in for a bite to eat and a couple of beers to wash it down, I knew I couldn't venture too far and it was back to my room in the hotel.

I just lay about watching TV, to be honest I was bored out of my head but I knew I had to keep a low profile, so after a bit of a doze I decided to go for dinner. I sat in the local pub, I had ordered burger and chips and a beer as well, just as I was about to tuck into it my phone rang, it was Porter.

"Where are you Jonny I need to speak with you?"

"I'm out Porter I don't want to be involved anymore," I replied.

"That's a bit of hard luck your having Jonny, you know the score, you will always be working for me."

"That's where you are mistaken Porter, I kept my end of the deal, you got Sam so that's us quits."

"Jonny our deal is off, we are bringing you in, now where are you?" Porter said quite angrily.

"You will never find me Porter and even if you do, I still have that letter that clears me of any charges."

"I think you will find Jonny that my officers are up in your house as we speak and once they find the letter you have nothing."

I laughed as I replied, "Do you think I am that stupid Porter? My letter is somewhere safe and if anything is to happen to me then it goes public."

"We can do this the easy way or the hard way Jonny, it is up to you, now if you want my advice if we pick you up you will get minimum time but you are going to have to serve some sort of sentence for being part of this or if I have to come for you god knows what will happen."

"Porter you are full of shit, I told you, I will redden your face if you decide to come for me I have everything in place to really blow this case wide open and once it starts I won't hold back, this goes right back to the murder at Belfast Castle and you ordered that."

There was a pause and then Porter spoke up, "Then if that's the way you want to play it Jonny, let the games begin."

He hung up even before I could answer, I slammed the phone on the table, I was furious he had sold me out and it was probably him who ratted me to Sam. I was screwed, the only way this would finish for him was my death, but I had other plans, I needed to go but I had to see Karen tomorrow night and then I could leave.

I lifted the phone again and took the back off it, I removed the sim card and threw it under the table, I couldn't even finish my burger and chips I was that angry. I gulped down my pint and then asked the girl for the bill, when she returned she said to me, "Was everything ok? Was there something wrong with your burger?"

"No it was fine I just couldn't eat anymore, I felt a bit sick." I couldn't think of anything else I just needed to get out of there.

"Oh right that's ok, I hope you feel better," the girl replied, as I handed her 15 quid I told her to keep the change, she thanked me and I left.

As I walked out the door I threw the phone in a bin that sat on the footpath, I think it smashed as it hit the bottom of the bin but that was it, I had no more contact with Porter and to be honest I didn't want to see him again.

I spent the next few hours in the hotel room pacing the floor, I was like a cat on a hot tin roof, every time a peeler car or ambulance went up the road with its lights flashing I got more and more anxious but my stomach was now telling me I needed something to eat. I was bloody starving so I took a chance and nipped to the chippy where I got a battered sausage supper with loads of salt and vinegar and a big bottle of coke, I wore a grey hoodie and kept it zipped up so nobody would recognise me but it didn't stop me being paranoid. I swear I thought someone was following me on the return to the hotel so I took a couple of detours and then doubled back on myself when I thought it was safe, I sat in my room eating the sausages and chips and they were really tasty. I looked at my watch and it read 10.30pm, when I finished my chips I decided to just go to bed, I got undressed and lay under the covers listening to the rain beat off the window and the hustle and bustle of the busy road outside. I closed my eyes and fell asleep.

I was back as a young boy sitting at the dinner table with my ma and da and my ma had made a lovely Sunday dinner, I could smell the gravy and could nearly taste the creamy spuds. As I lay there sleeping I could hear my ma speak to me, she asked if everything was ok and was there anything annoying me, I could see myself sitting there round our wee table and I just smiled at her and told her I was fine and everything was going to work out for the best. She smiled back and leant over and kissed me on the head, as soon as she kissed me they were gone, I looked round in a panic to see where they had gone but there sitting in my living room was Norman, Jason , Paul and Jonty all of them really white and disfigured. I couldn't breathe, I could see myself standing up gasping for air holding my chest, the four of them just stood up and turned to face me. They started walking towards me just pointing at me and saying, "YOU, YOU, YOU." I had nowhere to run, I was trapped, their hands were all over me, grabbing me, pushing me. I tried to fight them off but it was no good, I fell backwards, the chair went flying,

I woke with a loud bang in my ears, I was soaking, my whole body was sweating, I was breathing really fast, I told myself it was only a dream IT WAS ONLY A DREAM. It felt so real, I calmed down and looked at my watch, it was 5.45am. I looked outside, the street was really quiet, a street sweeper was the only thing on the road and I stood and watch as it drove past cleaning the road. I gave a sigh of relief and got back into bed. I tossed and turned for a while and at 7.30am I decided to get up and get a shower, I stood under the hot water with my eyes closed, it was lovely, it was nice and warm, there was a container of soap on the wall and I pumped some out and washed my hair and body. I stood for a while under the hot water and just watched as the suds disappeared down the plug hole.

I turned the water off and got out, I lifted a towel

from the rack and got dried, I then stood at the sink and as I brushed my teeth I looked in the mirror. I paused for a second and said, "This is it Jonny, this is the day that everything changes." I rinsed my mouth and turned the tap off.

I got dressed and went down for breakfast, as I sat in the small dining room, I had a bowl of cornflakes with extra sugar and then a mini fry with a pot of tea. I enjoyed every mouthful and with the time now after 9, I had a bit of business that I had to attend to, if I was going to go to Spain I needed to get money changed and if I was to stay for a few months then I would need quite a bit changed. So I went back up to my room and counted out ten thousand quid, I would have to go to a few places to get this amount changed and it would have to be outside Belfast so I decided to take a trip down to Newtownards and Bangor. it took about 4 hours in total and 20 different places, I even stopped into Hollywood and two banks just to get the rest of it changed but job done, I had 15000 euro and that would set me up in Spain.

I had planned that I wouldn't fly and would drive down to Dublin and get the boat across to Wales and then drive on down through England and over to France and then down to the south of Spain where I would rent somewhere on the outskirts of Benidorm. I could get a job in one of the many bars but I hoped and prayed Karen would go, although that was a long shot, but I knew I had to see her and ask her to go.

I couldn't take my *XR2* so I drove down to Boucher Road and into a car dealership where I struck a deal on a red *Vauxhall Astra,* it only cost me 2 grand to change so it was well worth it. I did the deal and he even threw 6 months' tax on it for me, I lifted what gear I had out of the boot and put it into the *Astra* and returned back to the hotel.

I sat and had a bite to eat in the hotel bar just watching the time, it was like watching paint dry, 6pm then 6.05 then 6.15. It was dragging by, I knew Karen would be going to the Bot about 8.30 or so, so after I finished my dinner I went up to get changed and at 7.30 I stood in my room deciding to bring my gun or not. Standing there in that room at 7.30pm on what would be probably my last night in Belfast was hard to comprehend, was this what I had become? A wee lad from the Shankill now going to be on the run for the rest of his life, I decided to leave the gun under the bed and to be honest, it felt good going out not carrying.

CHAPTER 21

Closer

I went down to the hotel bar and had a couple of pints, Dutch courage I think and then headed out and started walking towards the Lisburn road and to the Botanic Inn where I knew Karen would be.

I caught my reflection in a couple of shop windows and by god I was looking well in my nice white shirt and jeans, really dapper, as I continued the dander up the road I caught a glimpse of two men who were a bit behind me. I slowed down to see what they would do and they also slowed down, "Ballocks," I said to myself, they have found me. I sped up and decided to go in to one of the busy bars on the way up the road, as I went in through the front door, I made a bee line for the exit at the back. As I pushed the door open it led into an alley way, I quickly closed the door and slowly walked up the alleyway and just as it met the main road again. I held back and just watched the two men both wearing black leather jackets and what struck me the most about them was they were like twins with their bald heads and build, they were two big lads as they walked in through the front door, I made a dash for up the road before they seen me.

I made it up to the Botanic without them following me and as I went in there was already a good crowd in so it was easy to fade into the background just overlooking the dance floor, I stood at the bar I got myself a pint and as I stood there just listening to the D.J I was able to relax a bit I knew the two thugs would be in and out of every bar trying to find me and to be honest they probably would think I would be in here.

I looked at my watch and it read 8.30pm, Karen would be here soon, I turned to order another pint. I said to the guy behind the bar, "Could I get another beer mate?"

"Certainly," he answered, as he pulled the pint I looked in the big mirror that was on the wall behind him, my heart fluttered, it was Karen. I saw her reflection and turned quickly, I had a huge smile on my face as I saw her walk in with a couple of mates. She was dressed to kill, she had on a lovely black top and black ripped jeans, I noticed her shoes as well. She was stunning, her hair, her makeup, she was immaculate. As I went to take a step forward, a tall tanned fella came walking in behind Karen and took her hand, I stopped in my tracks. *Who's this?* I thought. I took a step back, I was tight up against the bar, my heart dropped, she has moved on, I thought, my head dropped.

"Excuse me sir, here is your pint," the bar man behind me said.

I turned, I had a real bad feeling in my stomach, it was churning, I lifted my head and looked at the bar man, he said, "Are you ok mate, you have went a bit pale looking?"

I answered him, "Aye mate," and handed him a fiver, he turned and went to the till and rang my drink in, he came back with the change, I said to him, "Just keep it mate."

I was so deflated, I stood and watched as Karen and her mates got a table over across the bar, the fella was talking into her ear and she was laughing. I didn't know what to do, I just stood there at the bar holding my pint and watched as the fella got her up to dance, I stood pondering should I go over or should I just leave? I started drinking my pint and watched as Karen looked really happy when the song finished, she walked back over to her table, the fella came to the bar just beside me. I moved over a bit to let him in, he was a bit taller than me, he was wearing a shirt and a pair of jeans, his aftershave smelt really good. He turned to me as I shuffled over a bit and said, "Thanks mate it's damn hard to get served in here."

I didn't know what to say, my mind was a blank, I just looked at him and thought, this is the guy that my Karen is going with. I know it wasn't his fault and to be honest it wasn't Karen's fault either, she deserved to be happy, it was me. I had fucked it up and I could only blame myself.

I replied to him, "Yeah it's a busy bar." I turned to walk away and the guy put his hand on my shoulder, I turned back again, he said, "I'm Ryan, are you here on your own?"

"Yeah," I replied. "I was meant to meet someone but I don't think it's going to happen."

"Aw poor soul, have you been stood up?"

There was something about this fella that didn't add up, I stood on as he ordered his drinks, we continued to talk until one of Karen's mates came up to help him carry the drinks down, she looked at me and then said, "Ryan are you at your work again?"

Ryan took her by the hand and said, "You behave sweetie, Ryan is allowed to talk to a good looking fella, I never caught your name."

I replied, "It's Jonny."

"Hi Jonny, I'm Susan and don't let our Ryan lead you astray."

Holy shit this fella is gay, I didn't know whether I was pleased or raging as he was touching for me but I was actually flattered and now I knew he wasn't Karen's boyfriend, I was smiling from ear to ear.

"Jonny why don't you come and join us, you will have a good night and maybe a better morning," Ryan said as he winked and put his hand on my shoulder. I would have loved to go over but I was really nervous, I looked past Ryan and Susan and over towards Karen, Ryan then said, "Well good looking, what's it to be?"

"Thanks Ryan, I am flattered but unfortunately I'm in to girls, I hope you're not offended."

Susan then said, "Offended? Jonny you couldn't cut this one with a hatchet."

We all laughed and then Ryan said, "Well who ever she is Jonny, she is a lucky girl."

They turned and walked over towards where Karen and her other mate was, I moved on down the bar a bit so I could see Karen better, the place was starting to pack up. I ordered another pint and stood just enjoying the night, after about 10 minutes I decided to go over to Karen and say hello.

I squeezed past the people and made my way over, she was sitting with her back to me at a high table with her friends, her long blonde hair was down her back. As I got closer, her friends noticed me coming over, Susan nudged Ryan, he lifted his head and said, "Oh, changed your mind Jonny?"

Karen turned round, I smiled at her as she stood up and threw her arms round me. I nearly dropped my pint as I heard Ryan say, "Jesus Karen you don't mess about."

Karen kissed me as we stood there kissing, everything and everybody just disappeared, it was fantastic. I reached past her and set my pint on their table and just held her in my arms and kissed, we kissed which I thought was a few seconds but in fact we didn't stop until I heard Ryan say, "You two need to get a room."

We stopped and Karen said to me, "You made it Jonny, I'm glad you're here." She turned round to her friends and said, "Everybody, this is Jonny who I was telling you about, Jonny this is everybody." As they laughed I laughed as well, Karen then said, "Am I missing something?"

Ryan then said, "We already met Karen," and he winked again at me.

"Hello again," I said. "I haven't met you," as I put

my hand out to Karen's other friend I said, "I'm Jonny, nice to meet you."

She replied, "Hiya I'm Leanne, nice to finally meet you Jonny."

"Can I get yous all a drink?" I asked.

"Of course you can good looking," Ryan replied as he took me by the hand, I looked at Karen she laughed and off I was whisked to the bar. I got a round in as well as 5 shots, as we walked back through the crowds I nearly spilt the drinks it was like running the gauntlet dodging the drunk people dancing but we made it.

We all took one of the shots, we tapped our glasses together and I said, "Here's to our futures." As I necked the shot, I coughed, it was stinking, I got a laugh from everyone as they didn't even flinch.

Karen said to me, "Jonny you're a light weight," as she put her hand round my waist and pulled me in closer, she gave me a kiss on the cheek.

I smiled and replied, "It's not that I'm a light weight, it's just that yous are hard core."

Ryan laughed and said, "Jonny you have no idea, these girls are bunkers," we all laughed and Karen got me up to dance.

As we were on the dance floor, the music was brilliant, I wasn't much of a dancer I just sort of had the two step nailed down and moved my arms a bit. On the other hand, Karen was some mover, she really did love the music and as she danced my eyes were fixated on her, she was beaming. Her long blonde hair was moving from side to side and her smile could light up a room, as the song finished, the DJ put a slow song on, Karen moved in and put her arms round me. I couldn't even tell you what the song was, it could have been anything, I was so fixated on her and dancing with her, holding her close, smelling her hair. My heart was pounding, I could smell her perfume every time I breathed in, it was magical, nothing else mattered I wanted this moment to last forever. I think we danced for a few slow ones and then it happened back to reality, as we danced I looked over Karen's shoulder, I saw the two bald thugs walk in through the front door. My eyes widened, as I turned Karen to try and hide but I could still see them out of the corner of my eye, I watched as they walked to the bar, they were looking round, they were searching for me. They didn't even order a drink, I didn't know what to do, the song finished and I took Karen by the hand back to the table, I tried to sort of blend in and with Ryan being a bit taller than me, I used him as camouflage. Karen knew there was something wrong, she looked at me and said, "Jonny are you ok?"

I replied, "Yes Karen, just needed a drink." As I lifted my pint, I noticed the two of them head towards the toilets, I watched as they went inside. This was it, I had to make a choice, do a runner or stay and hide? My heart was beating faster and faster, a bead of sweat ran down my forehead and then down my cheek, I didn't know what to do, I didn't want to leave Karen again. As I looked round at the packed bar and thought if I just stay here, they would never see me, I took another gulp of my pint and just waited for them to come out of the toilets and then they did. As I looked over I swear one of them looked straight at me, I hid behind Ryan again and sort of squinted round him to see what they were doing, they stood talking a bit and then walked over towards the bar and ordered a drink.

"Shit," I said under my breath, they were staying, this was now a whole shit pile, I was stuck. If I made a run for it, they would spot me, I had to just wait it out and hope they would leave. I looked at my watch, 12.30am, "Fuck," I said, this place closes in an hour.

"Would you like another drink Jonny?" Ryan nudged me and said.

"Aye mate if you're getting them in."

Ryan laughed, "Same again everyone?"

In turn everyone said yes and Ryan went to the bar with Leanne, I stood trying to talk to Karen but trying to watch what the two baldies were doing, they just were standing there drinking pints and just watching the room. It was absolutely messing with my brain, did they know I was here, were they just waiting for me to make a move? What was I to do?

Ryan and Leanne came back with the drinks and Ryan said to me, "Jonny I was told to give you this."

He handed me a folded piece of paper, I was confused, "Who gave you it Ryan?"

"The guy behind the bar."

I looked over at the bar and the guy that had served me was standing directly behind the two thugs and looking over at me, I stared at him as he pointed to the two thugs and then pointed up to the exit sign. I opened the note, it read, *These two headers are here to kill you, if you need a way out, get to the back of the bar and to the exit, do it before the lights come on, I will create a diversion at 1.15.'* I looked at my watch, it read 12.55, I couldn't breathe, I felt everyone's eyes on me, I lifted my head to Karen saying, "Jonny what's wrong, what is it?"

I couldn't tell her, she wouldn't understand, I just said, "Nothing Karen, everything is fine."

She said, "You're lying Jonny," as she snatched the paper out of my hand. I just stood there, I was stuck to the floor, I couldn't breathe, I couldn't move. The beads of sweat ran down my head, if only I had brought my gun I might have had a chance but against these two I was screwed, Karen read the note and said, "Is this serious Jonny?"

I nodded, "Yes Karen it is, it's going to happen." I looked at her, she was in shock, her friends went quiet.

Ryan spoke up, "What's going on Jonny?"

"Ryan yous are in danger, I'm going to have to leave before this kicks off."

"Jonny you can't go, just stay with us, who is it that is going to try and kill you?" Karen asked.

"Karen I can't stay, you are in too much danger, these men won't stop until I'm dead. I have to ask you, I had planned to run away and I mean out of Norn Ireland, if I make it would you come and meet me if I send you the address where I end up?"

"Jonny are you serious?"

Karen was now in a panic, I think she had sobered up as quickly as I did.

"Yes Karen I have to leave, it's a long story but if I get to where I want to be, I will tell you all about it."

I looked at my watch again, it was 1.12.

"Jonny just phone the peelers, don't leave." Karen was now crying, my heart hurt, as I stood there I looked round at the bar, there was only one of them standing there. I started to panic as I looked round the bar trying to find where the other one was but he wasn't any where I could see, I looked at my watch 1.15, it was time.

I hugged Karen and whispered into her ear, "I love you Karen, I will get away and I will contact you, I want you to come with me but not until I get away from here."

"Jonny don't go, don't leave me again," Karen cried.

"I have to Karen, I have to go right now." I kissed her on the cheek and walked away, as I started walking round the other side of the bar trying hard not to let the thug see me, I used the other people in the bar to hide me.

As I got to the other side of the room, the guy behind the bar was there, he said to me, "You have been set up mate, go out the front door, don't go out the back way, the other one is waiting on you."

"Shit," I said as I turned on my heels and started to push past the people in the bar. I didn't even notice Karen and her friends standing, everything was a blur, I could just focus on the front door and as I got closer my heart was racing. I kept looking back to see where the men were but couldn't see them, I got closer and closer and just as I was about to escape, I felt a hand on my shoulder, it stopped me in my tracks, I turned.

"Going somewhere Jonny?"

It was the two hit men, this was it, I pushed one of them back but the other one put a gun to my head, I froze. I stood there numb, I was stuck to the spot, at that split moment everything went silent, I could see one of them talking but couldn't hear a word and then the one that I pushed grabbed me by the arm and the other one went round the other side of me and grabbed me by that arm. People around me started screaming at the sight of the gun, it was pandemonium, they forced me out through the front door and that's when it all kicked off.

As we went through the door and onto the footpath, the flashing blue lights were everywhere, I looked up as the whole road had been blocked off, there must have been 6 peeler cars with peelers all standing behind them pointing guns.

I saw Porter standing, he shouted, "Stop where you are and put your hands on your head."

It was like slow motion, as I stopped still, the two hit men had taken one step forward drawing their guns, as they started shooting, the peelers shot back. I fell to the ground holding my head, the noise was deafening, as shot after shot was fired each of the men fell, one landing on top of me and I winced in pain. The shooting stopped and everything went silent, I lay there on the cold ground watching the dead man next to me, the blood ran from his head and trickled over towards my nice white shirt. As I lay watching my shirt soak up his blood, I heard people screaming and running past me, I could feel the beat of my heart so I was still alive and then I felt someone pull the other dead man off me. A hand pulled me over onto my back and as I looked up it was Porter I heard him say, "Hold on Jonny, an ambulance is on its way." I was confused, what did he mean? I tried to answer him but nothing came out, I tried to move but couldn't, I just lay there watching him and then I saw Karen. She was screaming, she leant down beside me, I didn't know what was going on, I smiled at her she said, "Jonny hold on, please hold on."

I felt tired, I closed my eyes, I could hear Karen talking but I was cold, really cold. I was so tired, everything went quiet, it was dark, I couldn't see a thing and then I saw the sun. It was warm, I could feel it on my skin, it was nice, I felt warm again. I had to cover my eyes at its brightness but I liked it, I felt myself walking towards it and then I heard someone talking to me, I listened carefully, I recognised the voice, it was my mum.

"Jonny just come home, everything is ok now son, I'm waiting on you, just come to the light."

I started walking forward but I heard another voice, I turned and when I looked round, it scared me. I could see myself lying on the footpath and Porter standing over me, Karen had her head on my chest, I was confused, how could this be? Was I dead? I could hear my mum again, "Jonny just come home." I turned but couldn't see her, I turned back, I was further away from Karen and slowly getting further and further away. I didn't want to leave her, I had to get back but couldn't, I tried walking towards her but I seemed to get further away.

"No," I said, "I'm not ready to leave."

I heard Karen again, "Don't leave Jonny, I love

you too, I have always loved you, don't leave me."

I stopped moving backwards and in a split moment, I was back in my body and gave a big deep breath. I opened my eyes and Karen lifted her head, she said, "You're back Jonny, you were dead."

She hugged me, I smiled at her and said, "I love you Karen, I'm not going anywhere again."

I could see Porter standing there, he smiled and said, "Everything going to be ok Jonny, it's over."

At that the ambulance pulled up and two men got out and walked over towards me, I knew I would be ok.

CHAPTER 22

The Warm Sun

After a few months, I was fully recovered, I had been shot in the chest and was lucky to survive yet another gun attack. All charges were dropped and Karen and I were engaged again, we were making plans to move away and go to Spain to live, we had already sourced out a nice house on the Costa Brava coast line but it was saying goodbye to everyone that was the hard part.

Billy had organised a going away party, it was to be Saturday night in the club and we were looking forward to it.

Karen and I arrived up at the club about 8pm and everyone was already there, Karen's sister had decorated the club and had got a DJ as well.

It was nice being on this side of the bar for a change, Billy had hired a couple of other fellas to work behind the bar so he had the night off as well, he came over and sat beside me when Karen was up dancing with her mates.

"Well Jonny, this it son, a new life in the sun, I'm sure your looking forward to it?"

"Aye Billy we are, I can't wait to start our new life together."

Billy handed me an account book, "Here Jonny, this is for you."

"What is it Billy?"

"It's your money out of the locker, you couldn't leave it there, you will need it when you get to Spain."

I opened the book up, it had my name on it and it read £56,000, I was wide eyed.

"Billy I told you what to do with it."

"Yeah I know Jonny, but I couldn't, listen to me son, never come back here, go and marry Karen and have a wee family of your own, there is more to life than the Shankill Road and you have a lot of living to do."

I didn't know what to say, as I hugged Billy a tear ran down my cheek. "Thanks Billy but if I don't come back then you will have to come out."

"You think? No more hotels for me since you are just 20 minutes away from Benidorm, I definitely will be out, you will be sick of the sight of me," he laughed.

"Never Billy, you will be welcome anytime."

At that Karen came back over Billy stood up.

"Hello love, I was just telling Jonny here that I will

come visit when yous get settled."

"Of course Billy, you can come anytime, just give us a buzz and we will pick you up at the airport."

"Super love, that would be great."

Billy gave Karen a hug and went back over to his own company for a drink.

Karen sat down beside me, "Jonny we are really doing this."

"Yeah Karen we are, a new life together." We kissed and then had a drink, as we held hands and just chatted, Karen's dad came over.

He sat down he said, "Karen can I have a word with Jonny a minute?" That was her cue to get off side, I knew what was coming.

"Jonny listen to me son, you have been mixed up in a lot of bad things, I need to know, is my wee girl going to be safe with you?"

"Alan she will, I know I got involved in things I shouldn't have but I'm away from all that now, I just want Karen and me to be happy and in a couple of years think about having a family of our own."

"That's all well and good but what if things don't work out in Spain, what will you do?"

"Trust me Alan, we both want this to work so we will make it work."

"Fair enough Jonny, I wish you all the best and hope and pray the two of you are happy together."

"Alan we will, I love Karen and nothing will keep us apart again."

Alan always put a hard exterior on but deep down this was killing him, I swear a tear ran down his cheek as he went in for a hug. He coughed a bit as he let me out of his grasp and wiped his cheek, he shook my hand as he walked away. I lifted my pint and took a big drink of it, this was harder than I thought, I never thought about what Karen was leaving behind, it was easy for me, I had nobody but she had her whole family and friends that she was giving up. I knew then she really loved me and would do anything for us to be happy.

I smiled as she sat back down beside me, she kissed me on the cheek and said, "I love you Jonny Andrews and would go anywhere with you."

I replied, "I know Karen, I love you too and as long as we are together nothing else matters."

The night ended and a lot of people had given us cards, Karen put them in her hand bag, we thanked everyone for coming and for their kind words and gifts, as I sat there in the club probably for the last time, Karen said to me as Billy came walking across, "Jonny I will give you a minute, our taxi is outside but I will get him to wait."

"Ok love." I think she knew as we were leaving the next morning I needed to say good bye to Billy, I stood up as Billy approached the table, he didn't even speak, he just threw his arms around me, we stood there hugging both of us crying. It was terrible, we were both emotional wrecks.

As we stopped hugging Billy said to me, "Christ Jonny, look at the state of us two big hard men from the Shankill." We both started laughing.

"I know Billy, you are the only person I'm going to miss, you have been there for me most of my life."

"Say no more son, it's not the end, it's the beginning."

I knew what he meant when he said that, a new life, a new start and that was always what I wanted.

I said my goodbyes and wiped my eyes before leaving the club, I didn't even look back as the taxi pulled away.

Karen and I had booked into a hotel up near the airport, we already had everything packed and were ready to go so when we arrived up at the Hotel, I was surprised to see Karen's mum and dad sitting in reception waiting for us. We sat for about an hour or so just chatting and when they were saying goodbye, it was tears again, I bit my lip trying hard not to cry, as for Karen she was in bits and it didn't help matters that her mum and dad where in bits as well. They left and Karen and I went to bed, we lay all night just holding each other, it was nice, I couldn't wait for morning to come.

We had some breakfast and then the bus came to take us to the airport, this was it the start of our new life together.

Our flight took nearly 3 hours and then another hour to take us to our new home, as we pulled up outside, the estate agent was there to meet us, we were both so excited. We got out of the taxi and got our cases out of the boot, I paid the taxi man and off he drove, we both smiled as the guy came walking down the path way of the house. He put his hand out and I shook it as he said, "Hello Mr Andrews, I am

Trevor, we spoke on the phone, everything is as you wanted."

He handed me the keys of the house and then a set of keys and pointed over across the road.

"Here is the keys of your car that you wanted." We looked across the road and there sitting was a white *Ford Fiesta Xr2* with tinted windows, I hadn't told Karen about the car, the look on her face was priceless.

It was brilliant, she turned and hugged me, "Jonny this is fantastic," she was beaming, standing there in front of our 3 bedroom house in a wee street just outside Benidorm.

I reached into my bag and lifted the Euros out to pay him. "I take it the transfer went through for the house as well Trevor?"

"Yes Mr Andrews yous are now the proud owners of this beautiful home," he ushered us up the path and into the house, as we walked in it was really lovely, every floor was tiled, there were a few dodgy pictures and ornaments but other than that it was perfect.

That night we went down to the local shopping mall for dinner, as we walked round the place, there were about 10 different restaurants and bars to choose from but we picked a place overlooking the beach and as we sat there having a drink waiting on our food to come, Karen said to me, "Jonny we could be really happy here."

"I know Karen we will."

Printed in Great Britain
by Amazon